RAWHIDE RIDER

Seasoned gunfighter Rawhide Jones quits working for Diamond Jim Brady to start a new life as a lawman, far from Laredo, in the border town of Santa Maria. But Brady sets his gunmen on Jones's trail to kill him: nobody quits Diamond Jim Brady and lives to tell the tale. Can Rawhide Jones turn the tables on his evil boss? With the help of Marshal Ethan Parker and his two sons, Jones tries to do the impossible and live.

DALE MIKE ROGERS

RAWHIDE RIDER

Complete and Unabridged

LINFORD
Leicester

First published in Great Britain in 2009 by
Robert Hale Limited
London

First Linford Edition
published 2009
by arrangement with
Robert Hale Limited
London

British Library CIP Data

Rogers, Dale Mike.
   Rawhide rider. - - (Linford western library)
   1. Western stories.
   2. Large type books.
   I. Title II. Series
   823.9′2–dc22

ISBN 978–1–84782–891–0

Published by
F. A. Thorpe (Publishing)
Anstey, Leicestershire

Set by Words & Graphics Ltd.
Anstey, Leicestershire
Printed and bound in Great Britain by
T. J. International Ltd., Padstow, Cornwall

This book is printed on acid-free paper

Dedicated to my parents
Olive and Denis.
When I was a child not all my
heroes were cowboys.

Prologue

Each of us has a destiny which however much we try, we cannot alter. Some say it is carved into the granite of time itself and is impossible to avoid. Our entire life has already been determined by a far higher power than we could ever imagine, even in our greatest of dreams. One man had attempted to change the course he had chosen for himself knowing that somewhere in the aftermath of the brutal war in which he had served, he had gone wrong.

Rawhide Jones's life had become soiled. Soiled by the war and the things it had taught him. He had learned to become a killer and, when the conflict was over, he had continued to exploit that bloody skill.

There had been a time when he had been proud. Now that pride had dissolved into shame. It had started out innocently enough when he had been hired to protect a wealthy Laredo man from enemies who were determined to kill for reasons unknown to Jones. He had thought of himself as some sort of ancient champion. Then, as one year drifted into another and then another, it became obvious that he was expected not just to protect but to kill anyone the wealthy man aimed a finger at.

In his thoughts Jones knew that being a hired gunfighter was not what he had been meant to be. He knew that he should be an upholder of the law and protect the innocent, not destroy them.

But it is not easy to change trails.

It takes courage to turn your back on the profession in which you have become as expert, and seek out your true destiny.

Rawhide Jones had that courage, though.

Enough was enough. When the orders to kill become motivated by nothing more than your paymaster's greed and malice, you have to stand firm. You have to be true to your convictions and refuse to obey.

Even at the price of your own life, you have to refuse. You have to be true to the destiny you know is buried deep inside your sun-baked skin.

Rawhide Jones had made that first step.

Laredo was a town that had become infamous, like the people who dwelled there. A town where the scum of so many other states and territories had gathered after the war. It had managed to grow like a cancer over the previous five years as it rejected every attempt for law to establish itself within its boundaries. This was a place where the West earned its reputation as being wild.

Rawhide Jones knew that he had never killed anyone who had not drawn on him first. He had tried to be different from the other men who called themselves gunfighters. He would never just kill in cold blood as they did.

But at the end of the day, killing is

killing. However fancy the ribbons you tie to it, it is still killing. A voice inside the tall lean gunfighter had been nagging him like a bad tooth for more than a year.

Eventually Jones had started to listen to it and accept the fact that his destiny lay elsewhere.

Rawhide Jones knew he had to become a lawman. He also knew that there was a job waiting for anyone foolhardy enough to take it in a border town named Santa Maria. Its sheriff had been slain and nobody wanted the tin star pinned to his vest.

Nobody except Rawhide Jones.

1

It had all started with the toss of a coin. A golden double-eagle had spun up into the smoke-filled air above a saloon card-table from the thumb of the forty-two-year-old Rawhide Jones. The seasoned gunfighter watched as the gleaming coin rotated for what felt like an eternity. Then it began to fall. He reached out and caught it in the palm of his left before slapping it down upon the back of his right.

The eyes of the other poker players burned into the famous gunfighter. They were curious as to why he had flipped the coin but none of them had the courage to ask the simple question.

A simple heads or tails decision had started what would become a legendary life. One which would go down in the annals of Wild West history.

But none of the onlookers had any

conception of the significance of the fateful action. He had already thrown his cards into the centre of the green baize amid the poker chips and bills. Losing a hand of cards meant nothing to Rawhide Jones as his eyes stared at the coin before he slid it down into his vest pocket. It was a mere game and he was bored with games.

He was also bored with his increasingly pointless life. The dozen or more notches on the wooden grips of the guns in his holsters drew the attention of all who saw them. They were there as proof of his ability to survive.

Nothing more.

For a long time he had known he was on the wrong side of all he had once held dear. His entire life had become pointless and he knew that he had to change sides. He had to step out of the bad and into the good.

Jones rose from his chair, touched the brim of his hat to the other men gathered around the table, then walked out into the Laredo street to inhale the night air. He knew that the toss of the golden coin had only confirmed the decision he had made earlier.

He paused, lit a cigar and then looked up at the stars. So many stars. They were like diamonds and just as impossible to obtain. Their sparkling light was unlike the lamplights which were dotted all around Laredo itself. It still retained a purity only unseen gods could have blessed upon them.

Jones knew that by now the letter he had written to the town's most powerful man, Diamond Jim Brady, must have been read. He also knew that it would bring the man's other hired guns out after him.

For nobody quit working for Brady and lived to tell the tale.

Rawhide Jones wondered if he might be the first to buck the trend, or would he end up as so many others had. Buried shallow on Boot Hill.

He stepped down from the board-walk and walked down the long lantern-lit sand towards the livery stable and his waiting mount. The tall black stallion had served him well for more than five years during his existence as a hired gunman.

But now that would change.

The toss of the coin had decided that. No longer would he skim the law by plying his trade of doing other folks' deadly handiwork. Now he would try his hand at being a lawman along the border.

If they would have him, that was. Before the war Jones had wanted to pin a tin star to his vest and uphold the law. Then it all changed. The country had gone loco. He had chosen grey instead of the victorious blue.

Mistakes had come easily after that.

Now it was time to change horses in mid gallop. He had to try to become a lawman. They were a rare breed of men who were willing to risk their lives for more than just a big salary. When they killed it was for a reason. Not just because they had been told and paid to do so.

It was a job which paid little but might give him the chance to rein in crooks like Brady and bring them to justice. Jones knew how the well-dressed Diamond Jim had made his fortune and it sickened him. Although Jones had always managed to stay sweet of the law, he knew that many had suffered and died because of the greed of the man he had worked for.

Times had been so very different five years earlier, when he had been looking for a job and had bumped into the man who was to hire him at the price he asked. Jonas inhaled the cigar smoke and continued walking towards the tall wooden building. Even darkness could not hide from his narrowed eyes the whitewashed word LIVERY painted upon its weathered side wall.

Working for Diamond Jim had paid well but at a price.

He now knew that that price had been his soul.

Livery stableman Harvey Krell had seen Rawhide Jones many times. Yet he knew little of the man himself, only that he was reputed to be the fastest gun alive. That was a title many men with hand-tooled shooting rigs claimed for themselves but Jones had never boasted about his abilities. Jones spoke with few words and mainly to instruct Krell, who owned and ran the livery, on how to treat the precious black stallion he called simply Jet.

Little else mattered to Jones.

His tall figure entered the stable, then stopped. The lanternlight spilled over him as he looked around until his blue eyes located the well-rounded Krell. He sucked on his cigar, then held it out to the man who ambled towards him with a pitchfork in his left hand.

'Smoke?' Jones asked.

The stableman tossed the pitchfork aside, accepted the cigar and sucked in its smoke deeply. The expression on his face was of sheer pleasure. This was a brand to which he could never afford to treat himself.

'Where ya headed, Rawhide?'

'New places!' came the swift reply.

'Want ya horse?'

Jones nodded. He rested a hip on the edge of a water barrel and continued to stare out into the street of flickering lanterns. The amber lights glowed and stretched out into the darkness towards the edge of town where a solitary stone building stood amid so many smaller wooden structures. That building was where Brady lived, surrounded by servants and henchmen who catered for his every desire and whim. And Brady had a whole heap of desires and whims which never seemed to be totally satisfied.

'Kinda late to go riding!' Krell noted as he walked with the cigar gripped in his teeth to the stall where the tall black stallion waited and watched its master. 'Ain't it?'

'Maybe!' Jones muttered without looking at the other man.

Krell led the tall elegant animal out into the centre of the livery. He started to brush the horse down. Even in lanternlight Jones's mount had a shine across its black body few others could have matched. This was a thoroughbred and it showed.

Jones kept staring out into the depths of Laredo like an eagle watching out for danger. Krell looked across at the thoughtful man.

'What's wrong, Rawhide?' the livery man asked. He plucked a blanket off a rail, tossed it on to the high back of the stallion and patted it down.

Jones glanced briefly at Krell. 'A man gets older and starts to realize he's bin riding the wrong trail, Harvey! Reckon I've bin asleep since the war started!'

Krell paused.

'You sick? Ya sound sick!'

'Sick of killing folks for other folks, I guess!'

The stableman continued to saddle the stallion. He groaned as he reached under the horse's belly and pulled the cinch strap towards him.

'You got a talent, Rawhide!' Krell observed. 'A talent to outdraw other folks! Ain't nothing wrong with that! You ain't never killed nobody in cold blood! Even I know that!'

'Maybe not, but I sure come close a few times!' Jones sounded regretful. 'Sometimes you can force a critter into drawing on you first and when you're as fast as I am, that's murder!'

'What ya looking out there for?'

Jones narrowed his eyes again. He saw activity in the shadows down the street. Two figures were moving towards the livery stable along the righthand side of the boardwalk. They had come from Brady's house only a few seconds earlier. Jones rose to his full height and flicked the safety loops off his gun hammers.

'You shouldn't beat yaself up for doing what ya do, boy!' Krell pulled the cinch strap through the saddle buckle and secured it. He looked at the man two yards away from him. He knew that Jones's honed senses were locked on to something or someone. 'What is it, Rawhide?'

Jones waved his left hand at Krell without taking his eyes off the figures who were still heading towards him. 'Get my horse away from the doors, Harvey!'

Krell did as he was told. He led the stallion to the back of the large building and looped its reins around a stall post. Still sucking on the cigar he started back to Jones, who stood like a statue, silently watching and waiting.

'Trouble?'

'Maybe!'

Krell's rotund figure stopped next to Jones. His puffing on the expensive Cigar grew faster. 'Who is it?'

Jones continued down the street. 'Put that smoke out, Harvey! Unless you wanna draw bullets like flies to a jakehouse!'

Krell pulled what was left of his cigar from his mouth and dropped it into the water barrel. A hiss like the warning of a rattler filled both men's ears.

'Who are they?' Krell asked again.

'Ain't sure!' Jones answered. 'But

they're coming to get me OK!'

Krell moved to behind one of the high doors. He vainly tried to see what his younger companion eyes were fixed upon.

'You upset someone in town, Rawhide?'

'Yep!' Jones drawled.

'Who?'

'Diamond Jim Brady!' Jones said the name as if it tasted like poison. 'I kinda ruffled his feathers a tad!'

Krell paused for a moment and stared hard at Jones. He knew that nobody went against Diamond Jim Brady and lived to tell the tale. Yet if anyone dared to do so it would have to be Jones.

'What?' The livery stable man was scared. Even though he himself had never even set sight upon Brady, he, like everyone else in Laredo, knew of the man's deadly reputation. 'Ya upset Diamond Jim? How?'

Jones flexed his fingers above his gun grips and kept staring out into the dark street.

'He offered me a job and I turned it down!'

Krell gulped. 'Nobody turns Diamond Jim down! That's asking to die, Rawhide!'

'Maybe!' Jones eased himself up against the tall door and watched as two shadowy figures ran across the street towards the corner. Only twenty or so yards and a line of fence posts now separated them. 'You better take cover, Harvey! They're darn close and I don't want you getting cut down by bullets with my name on them!'

Krell cleared his throat. 'You sure?'

'Yep!' Jones stepped into the darkness of the stables and listened as the older man found a place where bullets could not find him.

Even though the streets of Laredo were filled with the echoes of people living their lives to the full, Jones could still manage to hear the two men who had secreted themselves down towards the edge of the corral. His hands drew both guns and cocked their hammers as though by magic. Jones had been a master of his chosen profession for so long that he could rely upon sheer instinct when faced by danger.

'Careful, Rawhide!' Krell's voice warned.

Jones said nothing. He headed to the side door of the livery stable. The stableman looked up from his hiding-place. The gunfighter had vanished like a phantom.

Johnny Crandle and Bret Hawkins were two of Diamond Jim Brady's top guns. Only Jones was considered better. They had worked alongside Jones for nearly five years but neither man knew him. Men like Jones were mysteries even to their contemporaries. The two hardened men knelt beside the end fence poles with their guns drawn and readied. They had seen Jones in action and were starting silently to fear the mission they had been sent out to execute.

Brady had given them one order.

Kill Rawhide Jones.

As they crept along the line of poles

17

towards the weathered livery stable they both knew that they had to succeed or die.

There was no third choice.

Both gunmen reached the last fence pole. They paused and stared at the wide-open doors, through which lanternlight danced in an almost mocking nature. Horses moved around in the grassy corral beside them. The animals were as nervous as the two crouching gunmen.

'Did ya see him?' Hawkins asked his partner. 'I thought I seen him come out of there a few minutes back!'

'Just tricks of the light!' Crandle whispered.

'I ain't so sure!'

'Look! You head around back and I'll go straight in through the front, Bret!' Crandle emphasized his words with the point of a gun barrel. 'We'll cut him in half!'

'This is Rawhide we're talking about, Johnny! Not some drifter! He ain't so easy to kill!'

'Just do it! Rawhide's the same as everyone else!'

Hawkins went to move when they both saw the long shadow trace across them. Both men leapt to their feet, spun on their heels and saw the silent figure standing close to the fence poles inside the corral. He had moved between the horses unseen and unheard.

'Rawhide!' Hawkins spat.

'Yep!' Jones drawled.

Feverishly Hawkins and Crandle fanned their gun hammers at the man they both knew could never be matched for sheer skill alone.

Deafening lead spewed from their weapons like fiery rods of white lightning. The darkness lit up. Jones turned his ample frame faster than the men could fan the gun hammers. Bullets passed within inches of him. Then he turned again, this time to face them square on once more.

Only the fence poles separated the three men.

A million splinters erupted from the

poles as lead ripped the wood apart. They showered over the tall Jones like a snowstorm but he remained unafraid.

Rawhide Jones had seen the doubt in their eyes, had seen that split second when fear cannot be concealed, hidden or bluffed away by words.

Fearlessly Jones raised his guns and trained them on his targets. Even with bullets blasting at him he remained silent and controlled. His index fingers curled and tightened around the triggers of his matched guns.

Both Colts fired at exactly the same moment.

Two lines of vicious lead went like harpoons into the pair of gunfighters. Jones knew his aim had been not only true but lethal. Both hired guns were kicked off their feet by the thunderous force of the bullets which had hit them in the centre of their chests.

Crandle and Hawkins were lifted off the ground and thrown six feet across the sand. A trail of blood flashed in the starlight as it marked the path the two lifeless bodies were taking. They crashed into the corner of the stable's walls like rag dolls. A sickening duet of thuds replaced the ringing sound of the gunfire. Flesh and bone in contact with a wooden wall had a sound like no other.

What was left of life had quickly evaporated from them in a mixture of gunsmoke and hot steam.

Leaving gore splattered down the weathered wood, they slid into the sand.

The echoes faded.

An awesome silence returned to Laredo.

From the corner of his left eye the tall man saw people flooding out from saloons, brothels and stores along the town's main street. He ignored them as his eyes surveyed the results of his deadly accuracy.

Every single man and woman wanted to discover who had disturbed their pleasures. None of them suspected that the answers to their questions were lying in their own blood beside the livery stable that stood at the very end of their town. A place where the smell of manure did not offend the wealthier of Laredo's citizens.

Rawhide Jones walked slowly away from his handiwork into the livery and went directly to his horse. He holstered his guns, untied the reins and mounted swiftly just as Harvey Krell got to his feet and stood shaking in his boots.

'Is it over, Rawhide?'

Jones gathered his reins. 'For now!'

'Y-you OK, boy?'

'Yep!' Jones replied. The black stallion moved with a fluidity few other horses could have equalled towards the wide-open stable doors. 'Watch out for Brady, Harvey! He ain't got much of a sense of humour!'

'You figure he'll try and take it out on me?'

'Maybe!' Jones pulled two cigars from his saddlebags and tossed one down into the large hands of the stableman. 'More likely he'll want me dead even more!'

Krell gulped. 'What'll I do if he comes here with the rest of his boys, Rawhide?'

'Tell him I've gone south to the Santa Maria!' Jones nursed the reins in his hands and smiled. 'Tell him I'll be waiting if he comes visiting!'

'What's in Santa Maria, Rawhide?'

'A star!'

Before the stableman could utter another word the horseman had stood in his stirrups and ridden out of the stable, off towards the distant border.

Krell raced to the stable doors and looked out at the dust rising in the starlight from the hoofs of the black stallion as it charged away from Laredo. His attention was then drawn to the other end of town, beyond the gathered crowd. Krell tilted his head and squinted. He could just see that the door to Brady's house was now open. Light cascaded out upon the buildings as a man screamed out at the top of his lungs. Diamond Jim was calling out to men who would never again respond either to his commands or fury.

Krell looked to the side of his livery. Smoke and steam still drifted up from the bullet-holes in the dead bodies. He shook his head and wondered who could ever take on the famed Rawhide Jones and survive.

The sound of Brady's rage grew louder as he repeated the names of Hawkins and Crandle over and over again.

'They ain't gonna answer ya, Diamond Jim!' Krell muttered as he pushed the expensive cigar into his mouth and struck a match along his pants' leg. 'Nope! They ain't ever gonna answer ya again! Not this side of Hell, anyways!'

2

Dawn had arrived and so had the procession which flanked the stone-faced Diamond Jim Brady. The morning rays of the sun flashed across the wheels of the buggy as it made its way down the long street from his magnificent house to the ramshackle livery stable. Diamond Jim Brady sat alone on the plush red leather seat. He was flanked by six riders. Few of the locals cast an eye upon the small parade, for fear of angering the man they knew was one of Laredo's most powerful and dangerous citizens.

Those few stood in trembling silence as the small company of riders made their way ever closer to the place they knew would give them answers to the questions which filled their minds.

Brady cracked a whip and thrashed his reins over the back of his chestnut gelding. The animal trotted and drew the expensive buggy towards its goal. As always Diamond Jim looked as though he had been groomed by the town's best barbers and tailors before embarking on the short trek.

The vehicle, surrounded by the six riders, pulled up outside the wide open livery stable doors.

'Krell!' Brady yelled. 'Get out here!'

Krell had not slept in the hours since Rawhide Jones had ridden away atop his black stallion. The liveryman had known that Brady would eventually come to his small business to find out why Crandle and Hawkins had not returned. Fear had a way of keeping even the most weary souls awake. Seeing the fire in Brady's eyes made him even more alert.

Krell walked out into the breaking sunlight and swallowed hard as he watched Brady step down from his ornate buggy. He knew that one wrong word might bring instant death.

Diamond Jim Brady inhaled deeply. Although Brady had realized that

Crandle and Hawkins must have come off second best, otherwise they would have had already returned from their mission, seeing their twisted carcasses lying in the sun still shocked him. He stared at the pair, who had already drawn every fly in Laredo to their stiffening bodies and felt his guts turn beneath his white silk shirt. He strode to them and held his left hand over his face in a vain attempt to evade the smell of death that had already started to rise from them.

His eyes focused on the two bullet holes in the middle of their chests. One shot each had killed them. Only Rawhide could have killed so economically, he thought. Brady turned and looked at the frightened Krell. He walked towards him.

'You see this happen, Krell?' Brady asked.

'Nope!' Krell gulped. 'I heard it though! Sounded like the fourth of July!'

'I know! I heard it as well!' Brady

nodded and looked towards his men. He snapped the fingers of his right hand at two of his riders. They dismounted and made their way to the dead bodies. 'I'm taking one of your buckboards!'

'OK!' Krell agreed hastily.

'What happened?' Brady muttered aloud.

Krell licked his dry lips. 'They come on after Rawhide and he saw them! He went out from the stable and killed them! I figure they opened up on him before he finished them off!'

The elegant man shrugged. 'Damn it all! Jones must be even better than I thought he was!'

Two of Brady's men dragged the rigid bodies to one of Krell's buckboards and dropped them on to the flatbed. They rocked like statues in their death poses.

Diamond Jim stepped closer to the sweating Krell. He leaned over him and stared down into his eyes.

'Where'd he go, old-timer?'

'Santa Maria, Mr Brady!' Krell answered quickly. 'He told me he was headed there to become a lawman!'

Brady's eyes widened. 'What? A lawman?'

Krell nodded frantically. 'That's the truth! That's what he told me! He was sure acting strange!'

Brady rubbed his neck and glanced at his men. He then returned his attention to the livery stable owner and rested a hand upon Krell's shoulder. 'You telling me, the truth?'

'Honest Injun!' Krell nodded even more rapidly. 'It weren't no secret! He told me to tell ya! Rawhide wanted ya to know!'

Brady removed his hand and walked thoughtfully back to his buggy. He said nothing as one of his men remounted his horse and the other clambered up on to the driver's seat of the buckboard.

'Reckon Rawhide must have gotten religion if he's trying to become a lawman, boys!' Brady announced as he stepped back up on to his buggy. He gathered up his reins in his hands. 'Trouble with men that get religion is that they kinda expect to be crucified! Reckon we better not disappoint him!'

Diamond Jim slapped the reins down across the back of his chestnut and the buggy started to move.

Krell felt his heart beating like an Apache war drum inside his shirt.

'I'm sorry, Mr Brady!'

'Nothing for you to be sorry about, Krell!' Brady smiled and steered his buggy full circle. 'Rawhide did this and it'll be him who pays the price!'

The livery stable man watched the buggy and buckboard start back towards the heart of town, flanked by Brady's heavily armed horsemen. Sighing with relief, Krell walked back into the stable, dipped his face and head into a water barrel and then shook himself like a hound dog.

He was still alive, and that surprised the rotund man.

Somehow he was still alive.

3

As the day grew older dust swirled around the wooden buildings that surrounded the only stone-built house in Laredo. The vicious sun was beginning to sap the moisture from everything its merciless rays fell upon, but for one man it might as well still have been nightfall. He neither noticed nor cared. There were other things on his mind.

Rawhide Jones was still alive.

Brady had not uttered a solitary word since returning to his lavish home more than an hour earlier. He had just swallowed one brandy after another and brooded as his temper grew like a forest fire.

Most men would have cared little if their hired help quit, but not Diamond Jim. He had a reason to be troubled, for each of the men he hired to do his dirty work knew something to a greater or lesser degree, about his business practices.

Unfortunately Rawhide Jones knew everything there was to know and that made him dangerous. For Jones had been there from the very beginning and knew every small detail of each of the steps Brady had taken to reach his present position. To Diamond Jim it was like having an enemy know the combination to your safe. There was no telling what Rawhide Jones could or would do with the information he had accumulated over the previous half-decade.

In the past a few other men had known almost as much about Brady and had decided to quit. They had all been eliminated swiftly and without mercy within hours of their ultimate mistake.

Brady knew Rawhide Jones would have to suffer the same fate or he would never be safe. Never be able to sleep at night without fearing what the next day might bring.

Diamond Jim Brady placed the crystal tumbler down next to the tray of decanters and swung on his heels. All his men were in the large room facing him. None of them had spoken whilst their boss was raging around in his ever darkening mood.

Lonesome Hart was new to the team of hardened men who made their living by means of their prowess with their six-guns. He sat away from the other five and watched. Frank McHale was now the oldest of the men after Hawkins had been killed. Another blond young man with blue eyes smiled all the time. Yet his innocent looks belied the fact that he was deadly and had already killed over thirty men, women and children in his brief nineteen years of life. He was called simply Montana. Kyle James, Brad Dare and Eli Swift were the solid backbone of the team. They had all been working for Brady for two years. They did what they were told without question.

All of them watched. None spoke.

'Santa Maria!' Brady exclaimed loudly. 'Anybody know anything about Santa Maria? Where the hell is it?'

'It's an old Mex town!' McHale answered. 'American now but still more Mex than Tex, boss! I've bin there a couple of times! A lotta money flows in and out of that town from the cattle ranches!'

Brady shook his head and walked around the seated men like a general inspecting his troops.

'On the border?'

'Yep!' McHale nodded.

'Why would Rawhide go there?' Brady questioned.

Lonesome Hart suddenly came to life.

'Their sheriff got himself killed!' Hart said in a low, husky voice. 'There's a star waiting to be pinned on anyone loco enough to wear it down there!'

Brady walked to his newest recruit. 'How'd you know this, Lonesome?'

Hart tilted his head back and stared

with eyes that were always half closed. A smile traced his whiskered features.

'Coz I'm the one who killed the sheriff, Diamond Jim!'

Each of the other gunfighters turned their heads and stared at the man who had barely spoken a word since they had first encountered him a few weeks earlier.

'Why?' Dare asked.

Hart shrugged. 'I like killing folks with stars pinned to their chests! Makes me feel good! Anything wrong with that?'

Brad Dare shook his head. 'Nope!'

Diamond Jim leaned over the chair that Hart was sitting on and looked hard into his face. 'How many lawmen you killed in total, Lonesome?'

Hart's expression did not alter. 'Hell! I stopped counting years back!'

'You ain't wanted are you?' Brady asked.

'Nope!'

'Good! That's good!' Brady went back to the table and lifted his glass. He finished off the brandy in its bowl and inhaled deeply. 'We gotta draw the line at having outlaws on the payroll!'

Hart gave an amused grunt and pulled the brim of his Stetson down over his face.

'We letting Rawhide go, Diamond Jim?' James wondered.

Brady stared at the gunman in disbelief at the question. 'What? Are you serious, Kyle?'

'I always liked Rawhide!' James added.

Eli Swift nudged James in the arm. 'He killed Bret and Johnny, Kyle! He gotta pay for that!'

'He only killed them coz they was trying to kill him!' James said. 'I'd have shot the bastards if'n they'd started shooting at me!'

'He's a dead man!' Brady growled waving a hand at the six gunfighters like a magician casting a spell. 'Rawhide Jones is a dead man! You will see to that!'

'Why?' Lonesome Hart got to his feet

and adjusted his gunbelt. 'Why do we have to kill him?'

Brady stared at the tall ruthless figure. 'I thought you liked killing men with stars on their chests, Lonesome! Well that's what Rawhide will have once he gets to Santa Maria, boy! A big shiny tin star! They'll hire him and you'll kill him!'

Hart smiled wide.

'Stars make a real good target!'

The rest of the men rose to their feet and shuffled across the floor towards the man who was filling glasses with his best whiskey.

'He has to die!' Brady repeated.

Lonesome Hart accepted a glass of whiskey and downed it in one swallow. He smiled and held the glass out to his employer to be refilled.

'You're supplying the bullets and rye! Consider him dead!'

4

This was uncharted territory for the lone rider who rode with the blazing sun upon his back. Mile after endless mile he drove his lathered-up stallion deeper into the furnace of heat-haze mirages. Only a land created by the Devil himself could have been so hot, the horseman thought. This was a place where it seemed impossible to live and yet he knew that life did somehow manage to exist all around him. Death awaited the unwary on this prairie of shimmering illusions. Yet he drove on across the sand littered with sagebrush until there was only sand beneath the hoofs of his faithful mount.

Rawhide Jones was tired. Dog tired. Yet his horse still moved on as if knowing that to stop here for any length of time would kill them both.

A dust-caked Jones dragged his reins

to his chest and slowed the powerful stallion beneath him as he reached the crest of a high sandy ridge which rose to his right, towards a mesa of towering spires.

Something had alerted his keen instincts a few miles from where he now steadied his mount. Something which he knew was the last thing he needed right now.

The black horse turned in a circle as it fought against the taut reins in its master's gloved hands. Jones kept staring at the blue afternoon sky which was almost cloudless apart from a thin line of smoke which curled up into the heavens from the mesa a few miles ahead.

'War smoke! We don't need that, Jet boy!' Jones said.

He knew that there had been trouble along the border for years as various Apache chiefs vainly attempted to reclaim the land which had once been entirely theirs. Jones glanced back. The hoof tracks of his horse were the only thing which had disturbed the virgin sand for probably weeks. He squinted hard to try and see if he were being followed but there was no sign of anyone. Jones knew that when they did come after him they would have no problem. A blind man could follow the trail he had left in the otherwise smooth sand.

Again the horse turned.

The landscape ahead was different from any he had ever seen before: nothing like Laredo or the battlefields further north. It seemed impossible that so much sand could exist anywhere. But it did.

He raised his collar against the sun but there was no mercy from its rays. This was a land he thought was only fit for a man's nightmares. It was obvious that God had not had any part in its making.

Jones sighed and tried to rub the sand from his burned features. It only made matters worse. Now his flaking skin felt as though a branding-iron had been taken to it.

It had grown hotter the further south he had ridden. Now with the sun almost directly overhead it had become unbearable. He needed to find water fast. But where? The question screamed into his mind like a dagger. Jones swung his horse around until he was staring straight at the high mesa again.

The smoke was a series of plumes.

He had heard tales of how the Indians spoke to one another over vast distances. How they could send messages faster than the telegraph without a word ever being uttered.

Someone had spotted his arrival in this alien landscape and was alerting others. Jones felt the sweat trail down his spine beneath his already soaked shirt. This time it was not the heat that was melting him.

This time it was fear.

In his forty-two years he had never encountered Indians of any variety and that troubled him. Ignorance could be fatal.

He urged the stallion forward carefully along the sandy ridge, which grew higher as it rose toward the mesa towering above the prairie. The smoke signals continued to swirl ominously up into the blue sky.

Every few yards Jones eased back on his reins and stared ahead. Then, as Jet continued to walk, his master pulled out a scrap of paper from his vest pocket and studied it hard. It was a crude map drawn on the back of a Wanted poster that he had plucked from the bulletin board outside the sheriff's office back at Laredo. It had seemed that Santa Maria was far closer in pencil than it actually was in reality.

Jones knew roughly where Santa Maria was meant to be, but he was starting to doubt his own ability ever to find it. Then he saw that below the almost golden mesa there was a narrow canyon. He rose in his stirrups, shielded his eyes from the bright sun and squinted even harder.

A wall built by nature over a million

years blocked all other routes south. It stretched to both horizons in either direction. Again he looked at the canyon and gritted his teeth. If he were to continue on for Santa Maria he had only one choice. It was the canyon, otherwise he would have to turn back and retrace his tracks until he found another way to the remote border settlement.

If there *was* another way there, that was.

The doubts grew inside the mind of the weary horseman.

Jones lifted both his canteens and shook them. Only one had water in it. He was thirsty but knew that he had to give the meagre ration to Jet if he were to be able to continue onward. This was no land to have your mount die on you,

Rawhide Jones dropped to the sand and removed his hat. He shook the sweat from inside its bowl, then dropped it at the feet of the stallion. He unscrewed the canteen's stopper and poured its entire contents into the upturned hat.

As the horse drank the small ration of water the gunfighter panted like a tired hound. He wanted to sleep. His every sinew called out for rest but Jones knew that only death came to those who closed their eyes in this desert.

Suddenly something caught his attention again.

He slowly turned, rested a hand on his saddle horn and stared through the drops of sweat that fell from his wet hair. The haze tormented his eyes until his ears picked up a strange sound. He plucked his hat up from the sand, placed it back on his head and mounted in one fluid motion.

Rawhide Jones blinked hard and rubbed the sweat from his eyes. At first he was not sure what he was looking at. Then his weary mind managed to figure it out.

The images and the sounds became one. Apache yells and the noise of unshod hoofs beating across the sand suddenly made sense.

A score of riders were charging towards him from the direction opposite to where the smoke signals rose from the mesa. He grappled with his reins and swallowed hard. His throat was dry and there was no spittle.

He swung the stallion around and spurred. Sand kicked up from behind the powerful animal. Jet galloped down the ridge and headed towards the distant canyon.

Then he heard another noise.

Rifle fire.

5

Rawhide Jones stood in his stirrups as the mount beneath his saddle thundered at a pace he knew no Indian pony could match in normal circumstances. But the ponies were fresh and his black stallion was worn out. The rider leaned to his left, dropped his shoulder and turned his head. He caught faint glimpses of them through the thick dust that rose from his horse's hoofs as he tried to prevent them from catching up to him. At least twenty Apache warriors were closing the distance between him with every passing second.

Another rifle shot rang out.

Then a deafening volley of shots blasted through the dust and chased the fleeing rider and horse. He could feel the heat of the hot lead as it passed all around him. Jones slapped the neck of the stallion and forged on, knowing that the dust was his only shield. Somehow he had to stay ahead of it at all costs. There was no alternative.

The horse leapt across a broad ditch, steadied himself and then pressed on. Now it was the animal that was in charge of both their destinies. Jones hung on.

The blistering heat of the noonday sun was one thing but it was nothing to the heat he knew lay in a lead ball from a rifle barrel.

Jones drew the loose ends of his reins up in his gloved hands, then started to swirl them above the head of the galloping stallion. A sound like a swarm of angry hornets filled the ears of the black animal and drove him to defy his own weariness and find even greater pace.

'Keep going, Jet!' Jones begged his mount. 'Run, boy! Run like the wind!'

The valiant animal tried to respond but his long legs were now starved of strength. For more than half a day the thoroughbred had carried his master further and further south and now that long trek was taking its toll.

More shots rang out.

This time one came close to the left arm of the horseman, so close it ripped the sleeve from his arm. At first Jones thought he had escaped the ferocity of the lead but then a burning pain rushed from the arm to his brain.

The bullet had ripped through his flesh. He had no idea how badly but there was no time to check. All he could do now was keep riding and pray that no others would find him.

Droplets of blood started to be thrown all over the horse and rider. Jones continued to urge the flagging animal on through their mutual pain.

Again he leaned to his left and placed his full weight upon the stirrup. He looked back again. The dust was like a sandstorm as it swirled around behind him. The Apaches' cries told him where they were even if his narrowed eyes could not. He could tell that they were spread out wide, though.

They were like a living wall of death bent on one ambition.

His death.

Flashes of gunfire raced across the wide expanse as one Indian after another fired his rifle in hope of finding his target.

Jones eased his reins to his right and began to steer the exhausted animal away from where most of the lethal bullets were being aimed.

Like a locomotive running out of steam, Jet was slowing fast.

Fatigue was now taking its toll on the magnificent animal as it tried to obey the commands of its master. Jones returned his weight to both stirrups and stared at what lay ahead of him. He felt his heart quicken.

Something through the heat haze looked as though it might just be their salvation.

The mouth of the canyon was narrow.

Far narrower than he had first thought.

'Keep going, Jet boy!' Jones shouted over and over again as he leaned precariously above the neck of the horse, trying to take the weight off his horse's back.

Jones was balancing in his stirrups as his hands moved back and forth with the violent movements of the horse's head. Again he screwed up his eyes.

Ahead of him he saw something through the sickly soup of air moving in the incredible heat. Both sides of the canyon's walls were steep but there were huge boulders to the right. The horseman wondered how big they actually were. Were they big enough for a horse to stand behind and find sanctuary from the bullets which were flying at them from all directions? Whatever the answer he knew that he had to reach the boulders soon.

'Keep going!' Jones shouted. 'You can make it, Jet! You can make it! you gotta make it!'

Another bullet came close. Too close. He heard the horse give out a pitiful noise. It staggered for a few strides and then somehow managed to regain control as its rider hung on.

A chill raced through Jones. His worst fears had been realized. Jet had been hit. Yet courageously he kept thundering on towards their goal.

Jones rested one hand upon his saddle horn, turned and looked at the powerful rear of his black horse. A bloody graze at least five inches long was bleeding above the right hip of the tiring animal.

It was bad but Jones knew that it could have been a lot worse.

Angrily the horseman pulled one of his guns from its holster and cocked its hammer.

As his horse charged on toward the canyon, Jones fired all six bullets, one after another, through the wall of dust. Whether any of the shots hit their targets, the experienced gunfighter had no idea.

He returned the gun to its holster and slapped the horse's neck again.

'Keep going, Jet!'

A hundred yards later Jones reined in, dropped from his saddle and led the wounded stallion to cover behind one of the huge boulders at the mouth of the canyon. He hauled his Winchester from his saddle, pushed its lever down and cocked the mechanism into action.

He ran to the side of the boulder and fell on his belly.

Jones knew that he had to try and pick his targets.

He had only fourteen bullets in the long-barrelled weapon and he was determined to make each and every one of them count before he was forced to use the holstered Colt .45 which still had six bullets in its chamber.

There would be no time to reload.

He had to wait for a few seconds before he saw the first Apache rider break through the wall of dust and charge towards him. The Indian fired his rifle. Sand exploded next to the prostrate gunman. Faster than he had ever done it before Jones trained the

52

rifle on the pony-rider and fired.

The warrior was kicked off the back of the pony by the powerful rifle bullet. He crashed heavily into the sand.

Then the next horseman appeared, firing his carbine. He too was sent to his maker by one deadly bullet. Then the next and the next came howling and shooting through the swirling cloud of dust. They too were swiftly consigned to their gods.

Rawhide Jones felt the smoking rifle getting hotter as he counted his seventh victim hitting the sand.

Then they stopped coming at him.

Sweat trailed down his rugged features as he waited for what felt like hours but actually was a mere few moments of heartbeats.

The gunfighter tried to swallow but his throat felt as though it had been cut. He gritted his teeth and could hear the Apaches as they rode away from his deadly aim.

The dust cleared at last.

There was no sign of the remaining

dozen or more braves. He glanced back at his wounded stallion.

'They ain't gone far, I bet!' he drawled drily. Rawhide Jones was correct.

6

Since just before midnight the previous evening six well-armed horsemen had ridden at a calculated speed from Laredo with two packhorses carrying an abundance of supplies and water. Unlike the man they pursued, they were well prepared for the hostile conditions and merciless sun which hung over the baking-hot desert. Each man was an expert in killing like the rider they tracked. Each man knew that he could not afford to take Rawhide Jones for granted, for of them all he was probably the fastest with his guns. Only Lonesome Hart had not been tested and had barely known Diamond Jim Brady's previous top gun. Yet of them all it was Hart who seemed to be the most confident in his ability to bring Rawhide Jones's reputation to a bloody end.

During the brief time that they had worked together Hart had not given any respect to Jones. It was as if he had wanted the chance to kill the man whom his fellow riders all feared. They were alike in only one way: both gunfighters preferred to let their weaponry do their talking rather than waste words.

Dust floated up from the lethal caravan. It drifted before them across the hot sand and sagebrush, towards the high mesa ten or more miles ahead of them.

The riders had heard the blistering rifle fire clearly as they reached the point where the sagebrush thinned out and dunes of sand began. Hart, McHale, James, Dare, Montana and Swift dragged their mounts to a halt and stared out, curious, across the arid landscape.

A haunting sound of echoes washed over the riders. Each knew that a war of rifles had just ceased. They wondered why.

For a few moments none of them uttered a word. The silence which had followed the gun battle now hung on the dry air like a bird of prey waiting to strike. Each of them knew that it might soon resume but one question troubled them.

Who were fighting?

The only tracks anywhere to be seen on the desert floor was that of Jones's stallion. There were no others within sight of where they had drawn rein.

Rawhide Jones must be fighting someone, though. They all secretly thought that.

But who?

Hart moved his mount closer to the others and chewed on the tobacco plug in his mouth. His cruel half-closed eyes burned into his five companions. It was obvious to them all that Hart would kill any of them if he thought it might amuse or profit him.

'What's happening out there?' The deadly gunfighter asked, spitting a lump of black goo at the sand between them.

'Shooting!' Kyle James replied dimly.

Hart sighed. 'I figured that much myself!'

McHale rubbed a gloved across his sand-covered face. 'I reckon Rawhide's run into somebody who didn't cotton to his looks!'

'Too many rifles!' Montana muttered. 'Too many!'

'What ya mean, Montana?' McHale asked the smiling youth.

Montana glanced at the older man. 'Rawhide only got one Winchester but I heard at least a dozen or more shooting! He's got a bunch of folks trying to kill him!'

'Maybe they succeeded!' Hart spat again. 'The shooting stopped fast enough!'

'Old Rawhide ain't that easy to kill, Lonesome!' McHale told him.

'Any gangs around these parts?' Dare asked.

'Only fools and Apaches would hang around in these parts, Brad!' James said.

'Apaches!' Hart nodded. 'That must be it! I seen a whole pack of them critters when I was riding up from Santa Maria a month or so back! I killed a few of the filthy critters, to learn them!'

'No wonder they're fired up!' McHale shook his head.

James gulped nervously. 'I only fights white folks!'

Eli Swift lifted his sweat-soaked rump off his saddle and pointed at the far-off mesa.

'Look yonder! Ya see that, boys?'

'See what?' Dare grunted.

Hart turned his head, lifted his hand to cover his eyes from the fiery sun and then inhaled deeply. Again he spat a lump of spittle at the sand.

'Injun smoke!' he declared.

'I ain't going up against no Apaches!' James declared. 'I wanna keep my hair!'

'You'll do whatever I tell ya to do, James!' Hart snarled as he kept staring at the war smoke. 'If'n ya don't, I'll kill ya myself! Savvy?'

Kyle James nodded silently.

Dare sighed heavily. 'Maybe Lonesome's right! Maybe they already killed Rawhide and done our job for us! Hell, I bet they've picked his bones clean by now!'

'Ya figure?' James asked sheepishly.

Brad Dare shrugged. 'Sure! Leastways I hope they have! I for one don't wanna end up like Bret and Johnny!'

'Rawhide's good with his guns! Damn good!' McHale exhaled. 'I ain't never seen anyone who can shoot like him! Army man! They taught that critter good! Some say he was a sniper!'

Hart looked at McHale. He disliked the admiration his fellow riders showed for Jones. 'He say he was a sniper, old-timer?'

'Nope! Rawhide never says much about anything, Lonesome! His kind never does!'

'I'm kinda sick at the way you boys talk about Jones!' Hart snarled angrily. 'We're getting bonus money to catch and kill that bastard and that's what we'll do!'

McHale nodded and pulled out his tobacco pouch. He started to make himself a smoke.

'The problem with that idea is that Rawhide don't die as easily as most folks! I've bin with him when the shooting starts and seen what he can do and I'll tell ya now, if we face him one at a time, we're all dead men! Savvy, Lonesome?'

'I don't die easy either!' Hart snapped.

McHale laughed. 'I hope that ya right and I'm wrong! I don't cotton to being planted just yet!'

Montana smiled wide and moved his mount between the two men who were taunting each other.

'I figure that them Injuns killed him already, boys! Ain't no point any of us lathering up for no reason!'

'Let's feed the horses!' Hart stepped down from his horse and stretched his legs. 'Then we'll carry on!'

The men dismounted one after another. None had the guts to argue with Lonesome Hart. He was the sort of man with whom other men did not argue.

7

They ascended the canyon walls from both sides with the agility and speed of desert lizards. The dozen Apaches made no noise as they quickly made their way up to places they knew would offer them uninterrupted views of the man they wanted to kill. For them this was hunting. They were exacting vengeance for those they had lost to another white intruder a month or so earlier. Even though Rawhide Jones looked nothing like the bloodthirsty Lonesome Hart, it made no difference to the painted warriors.

He was a white man heading back from where Hart had ridden to and that, for them, was enough.

The Apaches had tasted the venom of Lonesome Hart's merciless bullets. He had killed simply for the fun of it. There were many men of all colours who destroyed for no better reason.

Jones had ridden blindly into their land and it was his misfortune that the lust for revenge was still burning in the hearts of the pony riders who roamed unchecked across the unmarked border. The gunfighter had timed his journey south badly and paid with the blood which still ran down his arm from the raw scar.

Rawhide Jones required a miracle if he were not to suffer a far worse fate. Death was the only certainty in this baking-hot place and the gunfighter knew it.

He twisted on the sand and studied both sides of the canyon walls which loomed over him. Sweat traced down his face from the hatband of his battered Stetson. Salt stung his eyes like crazed bee stings. Although Jones heard nothing his honed instincts were warning him. The sounds of the desert had fallen silent.

He narrowed his eyes and looked up at the rockface to his left. Bathed in the blistering afternoon rays of the sun, it was almost golden against the bright-blue backdrop of the desert sky. His head turned on his sunburned neck and his eyes darted to the high canyon wall opposite.

Jones studied it too with equal measures of desperation and grit. He did not want to die here on this unforgiving sand. He wanted to get to the border town and begin a new life. Death would only thwart that ambition. Yet for all his years he had never fought such opponents. The Apaches made all other foes pale in comparison.

Jones tried to think as they were thinking. Tried to work out their next move. He knew what he would do in their position. He would try to get above his chosen target. There was only one way to do that.

They had to climb high. That was what he would do. His head moved as his eyes searched for any hint that he was right.

Suddenly a few yards from the top of

the canyon wall to his right a wisp of dust blew away from the golden rocks. It had been disturbed by the moccasin of a man climbing. Jones gave a silent sigh. He knew that he had been right. They were doing exactly what he had expected them to do.

Being right was no consolation, though. It meant that the killing would soon begin again and he had had his bellyful of killing.

He wanted to tell the Apaches that he was no threat to them but knew it was impossible. Things had gone too far for there to be any hope of this ending without more blood being spilled.

Rawhide Jones slowly crawled backwards until he reached the legs of his wounded mount. He gave the stallion's wound a quick glance and gritted his teeth. He did not even think about his own blood-soaked arm.

Placing his spine against the saddle he reloaded his armoury of weapons without taking his eyes away from the great rocks which loomed over him from both sides.

'I'll bet you a bag of oats that we're gonna die here, Jet!' he muttered as his fingers expertly inserted bullets into the magazine of the Winchester. 'Me for some reason I ain't figured and you for grub! I hear they kinda like the taste of horse in these parts!'

Jet snorted as though he understood his master and scraped at the sand with a hoof.

Jones stopped. Both his Colts were loaded, as well as the hefty rifle. His eyes screwed up as his head kept moving from one side to the other. More dust drifted on the warm air from directly opposite. It floated from the very highest point of the jagged peak.

'Reckon it now depends on who'll get lucky!'

Again Rawhide Jones held the rifle in his hands. He pushed its trigger guard abruptly down and then back up.

He was ready.

8

No memory from his worst nightmare could have chilled Rawhide Jones as much as the sight and sound of the twelve Apaches who suddenly appeared on the very top of the peak overhanging him. They screamed out in language he had never heard before and started to train the barrels of their rifles down into the canyon at the huge boulders and the man and horse beside them. Only the shimmering heat as it played with the air between them gave the gunfighter a chance.

Jones grabbed the reins of his horse and raced to the canyon wall, beneath where the Indians were chanting their ominous cries.

Then the shooting began.

Bullets tore down through the dry air from every Apache barrel.

Jones raised his Winchester and

started to fire back. Bullet for bullet he somehow managed to keep pace with their constant firing. As the rocks around him exploded into dust under the impact of the hot lead, Jones ducked and kept shooting upward.

One Apache brave after another fell from the high peak and crashed into the sand around the man and horse. Then more Indians appeared on the high canyon wall opposite. They too started to unleash their fury. Bullets tore all around Jones as he blasted back.

'What the hell are these critters?' he shouted out. 'Why do ya want me dead?'

They were a formidable enemy. They seemed to have no fear or regard for their own safety. Even as he picked one off after another they refused to take cover.

When he had cut half of them down with his deadly accuracy he could not stomach it any longer. Swiftly Jones rammed his rifle into its scabbard, then moved to the side of the horse. He drew and cocked one of his Colt .45s, then pushed his left arm into the leather stirrup as far at it would go.

Kneeling, he fired his six-shooter across the stallion's tail and hung on with all his strength.

'Run, Jet! Run!' he yelled.

The animal bolted away from the rockface, dragging his master with him. The gunfighter felt as though his entire body were on fire as it was dragged across the hot sand, but he hung on and kept firing up at the Apaches.

More lead chased them but the powerful horse soon managed to get out of their range before he slowed and stopped.

It felt as though he had been ripped apart. Jones scrambled to his feet. Every sinew in his body hurt but he refused even to acknowledge it. All he could think of was his prized mount. He checked the animal again. The wound was still bleeding but he satisfied himself that the Indian's bullet had only grazed Jet's flesh and not gone into the sturdy animal.

'If I live long enough I'll sew that up!' Jones patted the horse's neck and turned to look back.

They had only journeyed a quarter of a mile up the narrow canyon but he could no longer see what remained of the hostile Indians. He rubbed the dust from his face and slid the Colt back into its holster.

'I wonder if they've quit, Jet boy!' he said aloud. 'Maybe their kind never quits! Maybe they'll go bury their dead and give us time to get out of this devilish place! Maybe!'

Jones looked along the canyon to where they had yet to reach and sighed. He could not see anything through the sickening heat haze. He shook his head, grabbed the reins and started to lead the stallion.

'Reckon we'll both walk and try and find us some water!' He started to walk even though his legs refused to stop hurting. 'There's just gotta be water around here someplace!'

The stallion snorted.

Rawhide Jones had walked only a few strides when a shadow from high above them traced across the sand several feet ahead of him. A man was standing with the sun on his back fifty feet above the floor of the canyon.

The gunfighter vainly tried to swallow.

His heart pounded as a million questions bombarded his weary mind. Were there even more Apaches hell-bent on his destruction? Would he never be rid of them?

Did he have the strength to continue fighting?

Then his narrowed eyes were drawn to the unmistakable outline of a rifle in the hands of the shadow.

He stopped. His chin touched his bandanna.

'And I thought things couldn't get no worse, Jet!' He sighed.

9

Rawhide Jones dropped his reins to the sand and gave a weary sigh. There was only so much fighting a man could do in one day and the gunfighter knew he'd almost reached that limit. He was tired but his gloved fingers flexed as they hovered at hip level above the grips of his holstered guns. The gunfighter knew that he had forgotten to reload the gun in his right holster after being dragged a quarter-mile along the canyon floor. He hoped that was a mistake he would not die regretting. His left gun hand had never been the more reliable but it was too late to do anything about that now.

For what felt like a lifetime he waited and watched the shadow. If the man above him aimed that weapon in his direction, Jones would have to draw fast, turn and shoot at a target fifty feet above him.

It was a shot he had never tried before. He felt the sweat start to flow down his spine again. It stung his bloodied skin and made him clench his teeth.

The shadow was motionless.

Like a statue.

Jones stared hard at it. He had to strain his dust-caked eyes in order to see the shape properly upon the soft sand. Something was wrong with it though, he thought.

Suddenly Jones knew that whoever the shadow belonged to, it was no Apache. This was a white man.

'You ever gonna look up here, boy? What's the matter? Scared?' A gruff voice called down. It echoed all around the golden canyon walls.

Rawhide Jones tilted his head. For a moment it was impossible to make anything out clearly. The sun was right behind the solid unmoving figure. The man was broad of girth and well built.

Muscular arms cradled the long Winchester. Whoever this was, he looked as though he could rip trees from the ground with his bare hands.

Then the man turned slightly and the sun glanced across his chest. The tin star gleamed and flashed light down into the canyon.

'You the law?' Jones called out.

'Damn right, boy!' the husky voice growled back.

'I thought there weren't no sheriff in these parts?'

The man started down the sandy slope. 'I ain't no sheriff, boy! I'm a US marshal!'

'My mistake!' Jones smiled.

'You through killing Injuns for the day, boy?' The question was aimed straight at Jones. 'I don't cotton to folks killing Injuns for no reason!'

'It was their idea! They attacked me!' Jones defended himself with spoken words. 'I never even seen an Indian before!'

The marshal seemed to accept the statement. 'I got me a reason for not trusting folks who kill Injuns, boy!'

'That is?'

The big man gave out a whistle. It was like the man himself, big and loud. For a few moments nothing happened. Then from twenty or so yards ahead two young men appeared, leading three horses. Even to Jones's sore eyes it was obvious that the two young men were Indians. Or part-Indian.

'Them's my boys!' the man said proudly. 'Their ma was full-blood Cheyenne!'

'They look fine!' Jones said.

'Got good hair!' The man laughed out loud.

Jones turned his eyes away from the two youngsters and watched the large man as he got ever closer. 'You gotta name, Marshal?'

'Yep!'

Jones started to walk to where the man was headed. 'What is it?'

'Ethan Parker!' The man said. 'My boys are called Walking Lion and Painted Tail!'

'Howdy, Ethan!' Jones pushed his hat back on his head and gave an exhausted sigh. He rubbed his dry throat. 'I'm known as Rawhide! Rawhide Jones!'

Parker nodded. 'I heard of you! Gunslinger!'

'I was!' Jones shrugged. 'I quit and was headed to Santa Maria to try and take up the job of sheriff! There's a crooked *hombre* back at Laredo who I figure I'd try and bring to book!'

'Diamond Jim?'

'Yep!'

Parker eyed the taller man up and down. It was as though he were inspecting a horse before starting to bid.

'Might be ya lucky day! I'm looking for a deputy!'

'Is that better than being a sheriff?'

Parker looked at his sons. They all laughed at the very same time. 'It sure is, ya young horn toad! It means you'll have the legal right to go after Diamond Jim! If'n you've got proof!'

Rawhide Jones accepted the canteen of water from Painted Tail and started to unscrew its stopper.

'You just hired yourself a deputy, Ethan!'

10

The wide river sparkled beneath a canopy of desert stars. Yet Santa Maria was a town which seemed almost asleep as the four horsemen rode towards it. Few street lanterns and even fewer stores were illuminated. Only cantinas and a single saloon remained open to mop up the money of those who defied darkness to remain awake at all costs. Some towns rejoiced in not having the restrictions of the law on their shoulders. Santa Maria, it seemed, was the complete opposite.

For the majority, fear of being unprotected against the drifters and bandits who rode across the river into the remote border town was a sobering thought.

Parker and his sons knew that for some in this settlement their mere presence would have a calming effect.

For others who relished being able to do what they wanted unchecked and unhindered it might be different. But the marshal and his boys did not care.

'Where we headed?' Jones asked the gruff Parker.

'Sheriff's office!' Parker retorted. 'If'n it ain't bin burned down!'

The four horses steered a quiet route through the back streets before reaching the main thoroughfare. It was obvious to Jones that they had been here before. They knew this place like the backs of their hands.

'What's different about being a marshal against a sheriff, Ethan?' Rawhide Jones asked as his tall stallion walked beside the smaller mounts.

'We ain't restricted to one town, boy!' Parker replied.

Jones's eyes lit up. 'So we could head into Laredo and ram the law down their throats?'

Parker grinned and looked at the rider beside him. 'Yep!'

Rawhide Jones nodded to himself.

'Even a deputy marshal's got the right?'

'Yep!'

Jones said nothing more. He just smiled as the four horses reached the dark building.

Parker pulled his reins back and slid from his saddle. He threw the long leathers to Painted Tail and then plucked his saddlebags from behind the cantle. He watched as Rawhide Jones dismounted.

'Give Walking Lion ya reins, Rawhide!' Parker ordered. 'The boys will take the horses to the livery and fix this tall black beauty up!'

Reluctantly Rawhide Jones did as he was told but he could not hide the troubled expression carved into his bloodied features. If he had one valued possession, it was the stallion.

'Don't go fretting none, Rawhide!' Parker said firmly as he stepped up on to the boardwalk. 'Them boys of mine know how to tend horses better than most doctors know how to fix wounded people!'

Jones nodded. He pulled his rifle from its scabbard, hauled his bags from the back of the saddle and then followed Parker up on to the wooden boards. 'If you say so, Marshal Parker!'

'Git going, boys!' Parker told his offspring. Like the obedient sons they were, the two long-haired youths turned their ponies away from the sheriff's office and led the two mounts away.

The riders headed across the street, down an alley and on to the livery stable.

When he could no longer see his prized horse, Jones turned to the marshal and waited.

Parker struck a match and touched the wick of a lantern hanging close to the office door. A flame flickered into life. Parker blew the match out, then lowered the glass funnel of the lantern and adjusted its wick. The light bathed over them both but only Jones's tall figure was not flattered by the light. His clothing was ripped apart and stained with blood from the countless cuts covering his body.

'And I'll tend to you!' Ethan Parker said gruffly.

'What?' Jones queried.

Parker pointed at the wounds and bloody bruises beneath the tattered shirt and torn pants. 'You might not have noticed it but you are pretty beat up, boy! If'n ya horse was in this state I'd shoot it!'

Rawhide Jones shrugged and glanced down at his injuries. 'I never gave it any mind, Ethan! Reckon I do look a mess!'

'C'mon, boy! We'll light that stove in there and boil us up some water!' Parker pulled a knife from his belt and pushed its long blade between the door and its frame near the lock. With a little gentle persuasion he managed to lever it open. 'I'll wash you down and make some coffee at the same time!'

They entered the office and closed the door behind them.

11

Night was the best time to cross the arid desert. The large moon had replaced the blazing sun and allowed the six horsemen to keep following the trail left by their prey. They had ridden for hours at a steady pace, knowing that somewhere ahead there might be Apaches waiting. Each rider had secretly prayed that Rawhide Jones was already dead. Each rider except Lonesome Hart. He alone wanted to face the gunfighter who had been Diamond Jim Brady's top gun for so long. He alone wanted to prove that he was better than Jones.

For the last half-mile the sand had been churned up, showing to keen eyes that Jones's quiet journey had turned into a frantic chase. This was where the shooting had started.

A group of buzzards circled with the blue moonlight upon their wide spread of wings. More of the large scavengers were rising from the sand ahead of the dozen riders and joining the others overhead.

The horses started to shy. Their masters held their reins tightly and kept the animals in check the closer they got to where the battle had started.

Frank McHale eased back and stopped his horse and pointed his trigger finger ahead.

'Look!' he said.

The other horsemen moved to the side of McHale. They too looked at the dark crumpled shapes which were littered across the moonlit sand.

'Dead'uns!' Montana said.

'Yep!' McHale nodded. 'But whose bodies are they? Maybe Rawhide is one of them?'

Eli Swift gathered the long reins to the pair of packhorses he was leading and stared Hart in the face. This was a youngster who pretended to be a man, he thought. A person who relished killing. A gunfighter who could get them all killed because of his own bravado.

'Ya figure Rawhide done got himself scalped out there, Lonesome?' he asked.

'There's only one way to find out!' Hart spat, dug his spurs into the flanks of his horse and urged it forward. The animal could smell the acrid aroma of death hanging on the night air. It did not wish to get any closer but the razor-sharp spurs gave the skittish creature no choice. 'C'mon, ya bunch of old women! Let's check these bodies out!'

It was obvious to all six that the earlier afternoon sun and the almost unbearable heat which always accompanied it had already started to rot the corpses. A sickening smell filled their nostrils as they all rode on.

Hart steered his mount to the closest of the dead. Gripping his reins in his powerful hands, he stared down at the body and spat again. Even the buzzards' tearing of flesh could not disguise the fact that this had once been an Indian.

'It's just a stinking Apache!' Hart said over his shoulder as the others closed the gap between them.

The riders moved on to the next crumpled body. This too had been feasted upon by the birds overhead. McHale and the others started to get edgy.

'I count another four out there!' the oldest of the gunfighters said, pointing at the corpses in turn.

'Yeah, but none of them is Rawhide!' Hart pulled his tobacco from his pocket and tore off a chunk with his stained teeth. 'I want that critter bad!'

Kyle James eased his mount next to McHale. 'I'm for heading back! There ain't no way Rawhide could have survived all of these Injuns!'

Hart chewed and stared at his fellow riders. 'We go on!'

'Kyle's right!' McHale argued. 'He couldn't have killed all of them! Not even Rawhide could get that lucky!

Look at the tracks around here, there must have bin twenty or more of them Apaches after him!'

Lonesome Hart spat a fresh gob of spittle at the older rider. 'There were more of the bastards after me and I killed enough of them! Nope! Jones could have outrun them on that stallion of his! We're going on and finding out for sure!'

Brad Dare gave a long sigh.

'Lonesome's probably right, boys! We gotta prove he's dead to Diamond Jim! We needs Rawhide's worthless carcass to do that!'

'And that's exactly what we'll give him!' Hart dug his spurs into his horse and started to ride away. 'C'mon!'

Against their better judgement the five other gunmen followed.

* * *

There was an eerie silence across Laredo. Although every saloon, gambling hall and brothel were doing big business it still remained quieter than normal. The echoes of the previous night's shootings still resonated in the memories of all who had heard them. Nobody wished for an encore. It was as if every single soul in town knew that the notorious Diamond Jim Brady was on the move. If fancy clothes made a man respectable then Brady would have been the most respected person in the wild town of Laredo. Yet Brady was more of a wolf in lamb's clothing.

His tall, elegant figure was striding down the main street with a silver-tipped cane in his left hand as his right rested upon the pearl-handled Remington gun on his hip. His clothes were handmade and imported from Boston and beyond. The black-silk top hat was tilted at just the angle that only dudes and dandies could get away with.

Yet Brady was no hapless dandy. He was a man who had enough cunning and brains to have almost taken over one of the West's wildest towns. Diamond Jim also knew how to handle not only his gun but his fists.

It had been a long time since he had started out on the Mississippi river boats as a young gambler with more than his fair share of ruthless ambition. The tall figure who strode down the well-illuminated streets knew that he was still more than a match for anyone who tried their luck against him. Whether it be at fighting or simply a game of stud poker, Brady could still get the better of most who dared go up against him. The few who had dared did not live long enough to regret their actions.

Success could be either earned or stolen. For a man like Brady life was too short to waste in playing an honest game.

Brady knew how to cheat, and cheat he did.

It was all down to style and confidence. And Diamond Jim was loaded with an abundance of both. He had learned long ago that if you looked rich then most folks thought you were rich. If you had the flair to fool them all, you always won.

As he mounted the boardwalk close to the line of gambling parlours he knew that every eye was upon him. Some feared him whilst others hated him. There were some who admired him but none of it meant anything to the man who swung his cane arrogantly as he strode.

Even though this was the first time for almost five years that he had not had any of his hired gunfighters with him Brady was confident. He seemed to sweat pure confidence from every pore and it showed.

Brady believed that his men would catch up and kill Rawhide Jones before the gunfighter could inform on some of his more illegal activities. Once they had done so it would be a simple matter to have them eliminated one by one.

His smile grew wider.

The swing doors of the brightly lit gambling house rocked on their hinges behind him as he steadied himself and gazed across the vast room. Few men could create such an entrance. It made females want to bed him and gamblers to want to wipe the smile from his face.

'Diamond Jim!' A voice called out from one of the many tables filled with poker chips and men at various levels of prosperity and bankruptcy. 'You want to try your luck?'

The tall man removed his hat and started through the array of green-baize tables towards the voice.

'Of course, Mr Mayor!' He beamed. 'I feel lucky!'

Apart from a tinker, they were all there, seated around the poker table. Tailor, soldier, sailor. Brady had spent years on the busy Mississippi river learning his trade and thought of himself as part salty sea dog.

Mayor Elias Proctor had once served in the Union army and had only recently arrived in thriving Laredo. He had no idea that the smartly attired man he knew as Diamond Jim was far more than just a gambler. He would eventually learn and it would cost him dearly.

Tom Conway owned the most fashionable tailors' in town and was always eager to please his best customers. Even if it meant allowing them to win a poker game when he himself had the better hand.

Silas Smith owned the most profitable hardware store in Laredo. This was something that Brady had wanted to add to his lucrative portfolio of businesses.

Four men sat watching one another with more than a little dubious apprehension. They all knew that each was a good card player but only Brady had the added talent of being an expert at sleight of hand.

'This is the first time I've seen ya without them men of yours, Diamond Jim!' Proctor said.

'Yeah, Diamond Jim, where are they?' Smith questioned.

Brady glanced around the table.

'They're around! They got a chore to do for me!'

'Ya wanna deal, Diamond Jim?' Proctor asked.

Brady smiled and pulled his billfold from his inside jacket pocket. He withdrew a pile of fifty-dollar bills and laid them down before him.

'I think you should deal the first hand, Mr Mayor! After all this is the first time you've played poker in Laredo!' Brady said as his cash was exchanged for multicoloured chips. 'It is your honour to begin the game!'

Conway and Smith nodded in agreement.

'I sure hope ya deal me a good hand!' Brady sighed.

'Excellent! I'm starting to like this town more and more and I'm grateful I won your support in the election!' The mayor picked up the cards and started to shuffle. It was not the best shuffle any of them had ever witnessed but they all smiled even more widely. 'I'm not very good at this, boys!'

'I've seen worse!' Brady lied.

'Yep!' Conway nodded.

'Me too!' Smith grinned. 'A lot worse!'

Proctor placed the shuffled deck down. Diamond Jim Brady cut them and then sat back and watched as the mayor picked them up and started to deal. Brady had only been required to touch the fifty-two cards in order to set them up exactly as he wanted them. Just one cut of the cards to a man who had the ability to hide an entire pack in the palm of one hand without anyone seeing them was enough. He now knew what each of his opponents would be dealt.

The cards started to spin clumsily across the baize to the players.

The game had started.

It would be many hours before it ended. Upon its conclusion one of them would be even wealthier than he had been when he sat down.

12

Lonesome Hart was suddenly not so eager to lead the line of hardened gunfighters as they steered their mounts across the desert sand past the rotting bodies. What faced them was something he recalled from his previous trek through this remote and arid place. The canyon walls rose up from the sand and appeared to touch the very stars themselves. They looked like something from a hideous nightmare with the rays of the moon bathing their rugged surface.

Hart eased back on his reins and slowed his mount. The five other gunmen caught up with him and noted the strange look carved into his features.

If fear had a look, it was on Hart's face.

'What's wrong, Lonesome?' McHale asked.

'Nothing!' Hart snapped back.

'Ya looks like ya swallowed a rattler!' Montana joked.

Hart felt the beads of sweat trace down his face and his spine. A chill overwhelmed him and he shook, but he kept tapping his spurs into the flesh of his tired mount, encouraging it forward.

'Cat got ya tongue, Lonesome boy?' McHale ventured with a wry smile.

'Shut the hell up, old man!' Hart hissed through his gritted teeth. 'Or I'll shut ya up permanent!'

McHale looked away from the nervous gunman. He sighed.

'Ya looks awful sick, Lonesome!' Dare said.

'This place is spooky!' James croaked fearfully.

'Haunted by the ghosts of a dozen or more Injuns!' Montana added with a laugh. 'Is that why ya slowed up, Lonesome? Is that it?'

'Rawhide sure ain't lost none of his shooting skills!' McHale sighed again.

'I've lost count of how many redskins we passed already and there looks like there's more up yonder!'

The horsemen aimed their horses past the large boulders and started into the mouth of the canyon. Again they were met with more dead Indians scattered at the foot of the rugged walls. An eerie silence filled their ears.

'This is where I got jumped by them Apaches, boys!' Hart said in a hushed tone. 'They came from everywhere!'

McHale kept his horse next to Hart's. 'Ain't no sin being fearful, boy! I once tangled with a bunch of Sioux and took an arrow in my back! Almost died of poison before I found me a quack to cut it out!'

Hart reached out, grabbed the bandanna of the older rider and pulled McHale closer. The moonlit danced in his crazed eyes.

'I ain't feared of nothing, old-timer!' Hart snarled. 'Ya hear me? Savvy?'

'I . . . I savvy!' McHale gasped.

Lonesome Hart released his grip and

then rested a hand on his saddle horn. He stared ahead as though in a trance.

'Never say I'm feared of anything or I'll kill ya all! You boys are wetting ya longjohns thinking about what'll happen when we catch up with old Rawhide! I ain't! I wanna catch up with that critter! Then I'll kill him!'

Suddenly from nowhere a rifle shot rang out. It echoed around the canyon. The horsemen steadied their mounts.

'What the hell was that?' James shouted. 'Who the hell is shooting?'

'Injuns?' Montana asked.

Then, right in the middle of the group of horsemen, Brad Dare buckled, slumped and fell from his saddle. He hit the sand hard, sending dust up over the skittish mounts. The five remaining gunfighters stared at the lifeless man in stunned shock.

'Brad?' Swift gasped.

'He's a goner!' Hart spat a gob of spit at the corpse. 'Took a bullet in the head!'

Montana drew one of his Colts and

cocked its hammer. 'Must be what's left of them Apaches!'

Hart swung his horse round and looked up at the moonlit rocks all about them. The horse continued to rotate as its master searched the high crags with his narrowed eyes. Then a plume of smoke was quickly followed by the deafening sound of a rifle shot high to their right. One of their packhorses made a sickening noise and fell.

Eli Swift released the reins of the stricken animal and then spurred his mount closer to the others.

'It can't be Injuns! Injuns don't attack at night! Do they?'

'Maybe not, but some bastard's shooting at us, Eli!' McHale dragged his own rifle from beneath his saddle, cocked it and brought it up to his shoulder. He stared down through the sights. 'And I think I can see him!'

The gunfighters held their mounts in check as McHale aimed and fired. His shot was close but not close enough. The unmistakable sound of lead glancing off rock rang out above them. Another bullet was returned from their unseen foe.

Hart stared at the sand next to their horses as it kicked up when the bullet hit it.

He looked at his fellow gunfighters. 'C'mon! Santa Maria is only a few miles past the end of the canyon! Let's burn leather!'

'What about the packhorse?' Swift yelled at Hart. 'It's got our provisions and water!'

'Leave it!' Hart screamed back. 'It'll slow ya up!'

Montana blasted his Colt up at the gunsmoke and then kicked his mount into action.

The riders spurred their mounts into action and chased the youngest of their number. More shots echoed all around them as other unseen riflemen started to open up from both sides of the narrow canyon. Red-hot tapers of fiery lead cut down through the night air all around the thundering horses as their masters spurred and whipped them feverishly.

Some bullets were swallowed up in the soft sand. Others ricocheted off the rocks. For each shot which came down from the towering heights, one was returned from the guns of the riders who were desperately trying to escape the attack.

The fleeing gunfighters were trailed by the packhorse until it too was felled by a rifle bullet.

The five riders spurred on.

13

Diamond Jim Brady cupped the five cards in his hand and smiled across the table at the only man left in the game. He had already seen Conway and Smith off and now had one more victim to pluck clean. Yet this was no mere game of cards like the numerous poker battles which had preceded it. This was a well-designed and executed destruction of the most powerful man in Laredo. The fingers and hands of the well-dressed gambler had done their magic and steered his victim into the trap from which Brady knew there was no escape.

Now it was a matter of feeding confidence into the mayor so that he would risk everything for the valuable pot between them. Most of the money in that pot had been provided by Brady. The fly was walking across the rim of the honeypot and it was only a matter of time before it would enter and be captured.

They say that you cannot con an honest man. Diamond Jim knew that was true.

Mayor Proctor held his cards close to his chest and returned the smile. He had accumulated over $2,000 in poker chips but it was only half as much as Brady had carefully stacked before him. What the mayor did not realize was that every winning card he had been dealt during the long evening had been carefully chosen for him.

Brady wanted to lure the politician into a false sense of security so that he could strike. He knew that there was only one way to take advantage of a man who wielded so much power. You had to own him lock, stock and barrel.

Diamond Jim Brady placed his five cards face down on the green baize and tapped them with his fingers. No actor could have matched him for looking like a man who was trying to bluff his opponent that he had a good hand.

There was already $500 in the pot.

'I'll raise you another hundred, Diamond Jim!' Proctor said as he slid poker chips into the already impressive pile.

Brady nodded. 'I'll cover that and raise you another two hundred, Mr Mayor!'

Proctor took a deep breath. He looked at his cards. The three aces were accompanied by two queens. It was the best hand he had had all night. He had won with far worse cards and could almost taste victory.

Proctor glanced hungrily at the stack of chips in front of the smiling man. He wanted them all.

'Your two hundred and another two hundred!'

Brady picked up his cards and faked a concerned expression as he bit his lower lip.

'OK! I'll match that!' Diamond Jim slipped another stack of chips into the middle of the table. 'And I'll raise you another thousand!'

A bead of sweat traced down the side of the gambler's face and dripped on to his silk shirt. Proctor smiled even more widely. He could smell triumph. He could sense that the famed riverboat gambler was not sure.

Or at least he thought so.

'You got a lot more chips than me stacked in front of you, Diamond Jim!' The mayor annouced. 'I figure you'll try and buy this hand!'

'I ain't that sort of gambler, Mr Mayor!' Brady said softly as he toyed with the chips. 'I don't buy pots! If you wanna keep going I'll accept your notes for the difference between our bank-rolls!'

The mayor suddenly straightened up. His eyes were gleaming in the lantern-light which filled the gambling hall.

'You will?'

'Sure!' Brady shrugged.

The mayor pushed $1,000 in chips into the centre of the table and swallowed hard.

'How much you got there, Diamond Jim?' Proctor pointed at the chips piled next to the gambler's five cards. 'Will you take my note to cover the difference?'

Brady sighed. He counted the chips and then stared at the mayor with troubled eyes.

'I got me over two thousand bucks here, Mr Mayor!'

'I'll cover it!' The mayor pulled out one of his calling cards and scribbled on it his IOU. He waited for Brady to push all the coloured chips into the middle of the table before tossing the card on top of them all. He then sat back.

'Show me those cards!' Brady said.

The three aces and two queens were displayed.

'Good hand but no cigar!' Diamond Jim Brady tilted his head, then turned his own hand over. The four kings and solitary ace sent the room of onlookers into a frenzy.

The face of the mayor was blank. It

was as though his mind had exploded inside his skull. Disbelief at losing with such a good hand had drained every ounce of strength from the seated figure.

Brady gave Tom Conway a glance. 'Cash me up, Tom!'

'OK, Diamond Jim!'

Diamond Jim stood and plucked the calling-card from the table. He slid it into his silk vest pocket and patted it. He tapped Proctor on the shoulder and started for the door.

'I'll be calling on you!' Brady told the stunned mayor.

Mayor Elias Proctor did not realize it but he had just been purchased for the scribble and signature on that little calling card.

He now belonged to the elegant gambler.

Proctor had been conned. He was a politician.

14

Santa Maria was still asleep. Most of it anyway. A million stars and a bright moon lit up the desert for miles in all directions. Darkness remained as the five horsemen neared the remote settlement. It had been an easy trail to follow but the riders behind Lonesome Hart were now troubled by the three new sets of horse tracks which accompanied the stallion that they knew belonged to their prey.

It was McHale who dragged rein first. His cohorts copied the older gunfighter and sat firmly in their saddles as Hart turned his own horse to face them.

'What ya stopping for?' Hart snarled at them. 'Another ten minutes and we'll be there!'

'Them tracks lead straight down into Santa Maria, Lonesome!' McHale voiced. 'But whose tracks are they?'

Hart kicked his horse with both spurs and returned to the four others. They were all skilled killers but each had their own doubts carved across their faces. Even the moonlight could not disguise their trepidation.

'Ya all chicken?' Hart asked. 'So Rawhide picked up a few strays back there! So what?'

'If'n chicken's a word for caution then yep, we're all chicken, Lonesome!' Montana said firmly. 'We're gunfighters but we kinda cotton to knowing who we're going up against!'

'I ought to . . . ' Hart's right hand moved towards his holstered gun. Montana was quick to repeat the action. Both men hovered in their saddles for what seemed an eternity.

'I wouldn't try if I was you, Lonesome!' Montana smiled. 'I might just be a tad faster than you think! Even if I ain't I'll put a hole through ya and then you ain't got no chance of getting the better of Rawhide! Think on it!'

'Montana's fast, Lonesome!' McHale said. 'He'll plug ya even if he's already dead!'

Hart relaxed and returned his hand to his saddle horn. 'OK! I know Rawhide picked up a few riders back in the canyon, but that don't mean nothing!'

'Maybe!' Swift shrugged. 'Kinda odd though, ain't it?'

McHale handed his reins to James, dismounted and knelt beside the hoof tracks. He was no scout but knew enough about horse tracks to keep his scalp in place in this hostile land. He stared at the sand and then looked back up at his fellow gunmen.

'I don't wanna get you worried, boys, but two of these horses were unshod!' he exclaimed.

'What?' Hart dropped from his mount and knelt beside McHale. 'Are ya sure of that, Frank?'

McHale pointed at the four separate lines of hoof marks.

'Look, Lonesome! The two in the

lead are shod! The long stride ones are Rawhide's! The other is a smaller horse but shod all the same! The two other sets of tracks are much smaller and they are unshod! Injun ponies!'

'Apaches?' Lonesome Hart asked. 'Maybe a couple of Apaches were tracking Rawhide and his new pal! Could that be it?'

'Nope!' McHale shook his head and stood up. 'These riders rode together! Even I can work that out!'

Montana leaned over from his saddle. 'Hey, Frank! Could two white folks be riding Injun horses?'

'That sound reasonable!' Hart nodded, rubbing his neck.

McHale shook his head again. 'I don't reckon so! This is something different!'

'Ya just guessing, Frank!' Hart grabbed his reins, poked his boot into his stirrup and mounted again. He gathered up his long leathers and sighed heavily. 'I reckon Montana's right! Two white folks picked up a couple of them stray Apache ponies left after Rawhide killed the critters!'

McHale mounted slowly.

'Can't be that way, Lonesome! Nope, it just can't be that way!'

'Why not?'

McHale turned and briefly looked back at the canyon a few miles behind them before returning his attention to the brooding Hart.

'I seen the tracks back in the canyon but didn't give it no mind! Them three riders who tagged on to old Rawhide were together! I seen the tracks where they had their horses hid out! Nope, they was all together! Real friendly like!'

Lonesome Hart gave a long confused sigh. He pulled out his chewing tobacco and took a chunk. His teeth ground it into a pulp. He spat.

'We're still riding in!' Hart said firmly. 'I'm still gonna kill Rawhide Jones!'

McHale drew his mount closer to Hart's. 'OK! But I figure we might have us more than one man to face when we gets there! What if they're pals of his? Maybe old war buddies!'

'You scared, old-timer?' Hart asked mockingly. 'Are ya scared of a man who cut and ran away like Rawhide done? Is that really it? Are ya just scared?'

'Yep!' McHale answered honestly. 'Damn scared!'

'Rawhide's more than one man can handle on his own but if'n he's got company to help him, we're all in big trouble!' Swift shrugged. 'Listen to Frank! You'll live longer if ya scared, Lonesome!'

'Trouble with you boys is that ya scared of dying!' Hart snarled and spat. 'I ain't!'

'We'll have to bushwhack Rawhide to beat him!' James remarked. 'I'm for back shooting the bastard and hauling his carcass back to Diamond Jim!'

'Rawhide's got eyes in the back of his head, Kyle!' Montana grinned broadly. 'Johnny and Bret found that out!'

'Rawhide's only one man!' Hart slapped his reins. His horse started to head towards the town next to the sparkling river at pace. 'C'mon!'

Swift raised an eyebrow. 'One man?'

'Not when he's got three pals in tow, he ain't!' McHale muttered to the others. 'Mark my words, boys! I figure Lonesome'll get us all killed before he's done!'

The four riders spurred and followed.

15

The door of the sheriff's office burst open violently. Both Parker and Rawhide Jones swung to face it with hands poised a few inches above the barrels of their holstered guns. Walking Lion entered, turned and stared back out into the dark street. He remained silent.

Ethan Parker lowered his coffee cup from his whiskered lips and looked hard at his elder son across the office. Rawhide Jones relaxed and tucked the shirt tails of his fresh shirt into his pants' belt. He then moved to the side of the marshal.

'Ya boy seems troubled!'

'Yeah!' Parker agreed.

'Something must have spooked him!' Jones added. 'I wonder what it could be?'

'What's wrong, Walking Lion?' Parker asked in a deep earthy tone. 'What ya seen, boy?'

'Five riders heading in from the canyon!' the tall youth replied. 'Got rifles cocked and sitting on hips!'

Marshal Parker glanced at Jones. 'Ya expecting company, Rawhide?'

The gunfighter inhaled thoughtfully. He knew that Diamond Jim Brady would not be satisfied with losing just two of his other henchmen to Jones's superior gun skills. He had to send the rest of them to silence him. To keep Brady's neck from a noose.

'I figured Brady might send someone after me!' Jones walked to the door and stood shoulder to shoulder with Walking Lion.

'Why?'

'Because I know too much, Ethan!'

'Yeah?'

'Yep! He tried to have me snuffed out back in Laredo!' Jones answered. 'I had to kill two of his boys when they tried to bushwhack me! I knew he wouldn't quit! I'm too dangerous to have running free, I guess!'

'I'd heard that Diamond Jim don't

like quitters!' Parker finished his brew, placed the cup down and moved to his rifle on the dusty desk. He lifted it and began to push bullets into its magazine from an open box of shells. 'He must be darn scared about what your knowledge could do to him, boy! Mighty damn scared!'

'I know all there is to know about him and his shady deals, Marshal!' Jones screwed up his eyes but was unable to see what Walking Lion had already focused upon at the town's furthest edges. 'I know how he's swindled and killed everyone who's got in his way over the last five years!'

Parker glanced up. 'That kinda information can shorten a critter's life, Rawhide!'

'Yep!' Jones agreed.

'You ever kill for money?' Walking Lion asked.

Rawhide Jones rested a hand on the shoulder of the younger man and smiled.

'I've never killed anyone who weren't

trying to kill me first, son! That's why I quit! Diamond Jim was starting to want me to just draw on anyone who was in his way! I don't do that sorta thing! Never have!'

'Rawhide!' Parker said.

Jones turned his head and saw the tin star flying across the room from the marshal's hand. The gunfighter caught it, then looked at it carefully. It had Deputy US Marshal embossed upon its shiny surface. He looked up at Parker.

'Does this mean I'm officially a lawman, Marshal?'

'Yep!' Parker answered as he continued to load the long-barrelled Winchester.

'Ain't I meant to say some oath or the like?' Jones asked as hw pinned the star to his shirt.

'Yep!' Parker nodded. 'Do ya swear to be a dumb-ass lawman like me and my boys, Rawhide? Willing to duck lead for short rations and even shorter pay?'

'Reckon so!' Jones smiled.

'Ya hired!' Parker walked towards both men. 'Pin that star under ya vest so it don't draw bullets! I've seen even the most sorrowful of gunhands manage to find the target when there's a star on a shirt!'

Rawhide Jones did as instructed.

'Where are they?' Parker asked his son.

The youth pointed. 'Down at the outskirts of town! They are close but ain't reached the hardware store yet!'

'Go to ya brother!' Parker pulled the door wide and pushed Walking Lion out on to the boardwalk. He followed with Jones a few steps behind him. 'Tell Painted Tail to get his guns, circle the buildings and try to get behind them five riders! I don't want no shooting, though, not until they open up with their weaponry! Right?'

'Right, Father!'

'Then you come back to me and Rawhide!' Parker added.

'OK.'

Rawhide Jones stepped beside the marshal's sturdy frame. They both watched as the young man ran silently across the dark street and disappeared into a side alley. Jones thought that it was like watching a puma.

'Are them boys of yours good with their guns, Marshal?' he asked. 'I mean, can they hit what they aim at?'

'Yep!' Parker turned the brass wheel of the wall lantern until the flame went out. Darkness returned to the sheriff's office porch. 'But they can be too damn trusting and a father gotta look out for that! They'd not last a day without my telling them what to do!'

'Too trusting?' Jones repeated the words.

'Yep! Too damn trusting! They don't see the black side of men's souls like I do!' Parker sighed. 'A man can get himself dead pretty quick that way!'

Jones nodded in agreement. 'It's a good trait, though!'

'Not in these parts it ain't!' Parker corrected. 'C'mon, Rawhide! You and me are gonna go find us some cover and wait to see what these riders intend doing.'

Both men moved quickly across the sandy street to where the moonlight did not touch.

They found a pile of empty beer barrels at the corner of a closed saloon and rested against them.

'Are these gunfighters fast?' Parker asked.

'Yep!'

'Damn!'

16

Lonesome Hart was no hero. He was a man who killed for money and the more money that was offered, the more he would unleash his merciless lead. The brutal kill was his forte. There was no honour or allowing an opponent to draw first with his breed of gunfighter. He would happily kill with a back shot as long as he was paid.

Hart did not fight. He slayed.

On their steady approach to Santa Maria he had managed to steer his own mount between the four other gunfighters' horses. He knew that if the bullets started to fly he would have a chance of escaping their lethal fury. His four weary companions had no idea that he was using them as human shields.

The sky had changed during the long ride down from the canyon and now more than half its stars were masked by black dangerous clouds as a lightning storm steadily closed in on them. Light had started to flash angrily above the growing clouds. A rumble in the air had alerted the horses that there was a storm brewing.

They were now skittish.

Almost as skittish as their masters.

Vicious storms were native to this and other remote desert regions. When the heavens awoke out here it was as though the devil himself was conducting every lightning bolt seeking out hapless prey to destroy. When it rained it rained hard. So hard that it could wash entire towns and their populations away in flash floods.

The five riders could smell the change in the night air. They had all experienced it before. None of the men wanted to be out on the desolate sand when all hell erupted above them. Santa Maria offered a little protection but not as much as they would have chosen for themselves had they had a choice.

The mostly adobe buildings had weathered many storms since the town had been created but there was no guarantee that it could survive a really bad one. When nature turned on those ill-equipped to withstand its venom, people died.

'Smell that air!' Montana said. 'That storm's closing in on us faster than I like!'

'All I can smell is Rawhide Jones!' Hart spat a lump of goo at the ground. 'And the money Diamond Jim'll pay us for his hide!'

'Montana's right, Lonesome! The storm's getting closer!' McHale said as he kept his tired mount moving with continual jabs of his spurs. 'We gotta get under cover before that thing sweeps over us!'

'We're almost there!' Swift piped up thankfully.

Blinding flashes of white-hot lightning forked down from the brooding black sky a few miles from them and hit the desert sand. Flashes of flames could be seen as islands of bone-dry sage-brush were ignited into miniature infernos.

Montana looked over his shoulder and rubbed his whiskerless chin with a gloved hand. For the first time for days he was not smiling. He, like the others, knew how dangerous storms were out here in the arid desert.

'I'm for getting into town as fast as we can!' he said nervously. 'I don't cotton to my hair being parted by no lightning bolt!'

'Me neither!' James agreed. 'Let's spur as hard as we can and get off this damn sand!'

'I'm with you, Kyle!' Swift nodded vigorously.

'Me too!' McHale added.

'Hold on there, ya yella bastards! We keep riding at this pace, boys!' Hart insisted. 'We don't wanna run from a storm into the barrels of Rawhide's guns, do we? That storm's a good half an hour from here! Ain't no rush! Just keep riding!'

'But . . . ' James stammered.

'Do as I tell ya!' Hart shouted.

The others had no idea that Hart's concern was only for his own neck. He was far more frightened of the man they sought than of the gathering storm. Reluctantly once again they nodded and kept their mounts moving at the same pace.

The hardware store was the first building they reached. It, like most of the other buildings, was shrouded in darkness. The horses were in line as the riders aimed them straight down the middle of the main street.

'Where we headed, Lonesome?' James asked.

'The closest saloon!' Hart replied in a low drawl.

'But everything's closed up!' Montana said.

'Not to us!' Hart spat. 'I'm thirsty! I'll kick down the first locked saloon door we find!'

They rode on.

17

The angry storm was gathering pace out on the arid land south of Santa Maria. Even the river became unsettled beneath the dark sky. A cold breeze gusted and lifted sand into the night air. An air which had the aroma of burning as lightning continued to mark its progress towards the small settlement. The thunder grew louder as it signalled its imminent arrival to everything in its path. Rawhide Jones touched the arm of Marshal Parker. He pointed the barrel of one of his Colts at the five horsemen who were making their way down the centre of the street. The distant flashes of lightning danced off the long rifles in the hands of the intrepid horsemen.

'Now what do we do?' Jones asked.

The lawman looked at his newest deputy and smiled. He had met many men in his day. Men who would have willingly started to open up with their weapons at the first sign of trouble but Jones was different. Jones knew in his guts that these five riders were gunning for him but he could not simply kill them. Rawhide Jones had a sense of fair play woven into his fibre.

'We wait and see what they do next, Rawhide!' Parker answered quietly.

'I know they're out to get me, Marshal!' Jones sighed as he toyed with the gun in his right hand. 'But knowing and proving are two separate things, ain't they?'

'Damn right!' Parker agreed. 'However much we want to kill them varmints, we gotta wait for them to do something first!'

'They gotta make a play before I can do something!' Jones said thoughtfully. 'I can't just cut them down even though I know that Brady's paid them critters to come and kill me!'

'Yep!' the marshal said. 'They gotta do something or it'll be murder in the eyes of the law!'

Jones felt a bead of sweat race a route down his face. 'And how do I know that my instincts are right without eating a bellyful of lead first?'

'You will, boy!' Parker told his companion. 'You got the makings and that'll bring ya through!'

Jones squinted. He could see the figure of Painted Tail walking unseen behind the riders. He looked at the marshal but Parker had already spotted his son.

The five horsemen turned their mounts and stopped next to one of the hitching rails outside a saloon directly opposite the pile of barrels Parker and Jones were hiding behind. The two law officers watched as the five men dismounted and tied their reins to the long pole securely.

'Looks like they're a tad thirsty, boy!' Parker commented as he checked the rifle in his hands. 'I like men who got dry throats! They kinda help ya win!'

'Them boys are always thirsty,

Ethan!' Jones said as Walking Lion arrived silently beside them. The youngster knelt and pulled his gun from his belt.

'The storm is bad, Father!'

Parker glanced upward. 'Yep! Mighty troubled up there, ain't it?'

'What should I do?' Walking Lion asked.

'Go and keep ya brother company!' Parker said. 'Don't do no shooting until ya hear my old Winchester letting loose! Understand?'

'Yes, Father!'

The son had received his instructions from his father. Before Jones could add a single word Walking Lion had disappeared like a phantom into the shadows. Parker crouched down against the corner and stared down the street with Jones looking over his broad shoulder.

Hart was first to step up on to the boardwalk outside the locked saloon. Defiantly, he raised his left leg and gave the door a mighty kick. Its weathered wood and brittle lock were no match for the high-heeled boot. It shattered and fell from its hinges.

Hart entered. The others followed.

'Now they done broke the law, Rawhide!' Parker smiled.

'Reckon so!' Jones raised his eyebrows. 'Do we go in and arrest them?'

'I'd give them a few minutes!' The more experienced lawman shrugged.

'Yeah?'

'Yep!' Parker nodded firmly and produced two cigars from his vest pocket. He offered one to Jones and bit off the tip of his own. He struck a match, cupped its flame against the wind which was picking up and lit both of the long smokes. 'By the time we've smoked these things them boys should have themselves a gutful of whiskey!'

'Reckon so!' Jones said through a cloud of smoke.

'Much easier to tackle folks who got a head full of hard liquor than it is to face sober ones!' Parker smiled. 'Mind you, drunkards sometimes shoot before they think!'

Rawhide Jones sucked in the smoke and went silent.

* * *

Lonesome Hart had marched through the debris of the shattered wooden door to the bar counter, which was made up of three planks of lumber perched upon two large beer barrels. After lighting the pair of lanterns perched on either end of the counter Hart rested his hands on his holstered gun grips and stared at the limited selection of bottles standing before a cracked mirror on a worm-riddled shelf. It was obvious to the five gunmen that this was a border town saloon which survived by keeping its Mexican patrons happy, Tequila bottles with their worms still lying in the amber liquor dominated the choice. A few bottles of whiskey remained with their seals unbroken amid a year's dust.

'I hate Mex liquor!' James snarled.

McHale reached over, grabbed a bottle of whiskey and blew the dust from it. 'Here, Kyle! Pour us a couple of shots!'

'They got any beer in this sty?' Montana asked.

'There!' McHale pointed at the wall where a beer barrel was balanced upon a rickety table. 'Ain't too sure what they might make beer from down here but if it's got suds then I figure it should wash the sand down!'

Montana moved to the barrel with a glass and poured a long brew. It looked like beer. He started to drink.

'Tastes OK!'

They started to help themselves to the whiskey and beer in the flickering light of the coal-tar lanterns. After a long hard ride anything would have tasted good. Anything to wash the dust from their throats.

Hart was the only one to try the tequila. He poured most of a bottle's contents into a beer glass and stared at the shrivelled worm as it spun inside the filthy vessel.

James leaned over after downing a shot of whiskey. His eyes widened.

'Ya ain't gonna drink that, are ya?' he asked. 'It's got a bug in it!'

Hart pushed his fingers into the glass and pulled out the worm. He tossed it into his mouth and chewed. 'I like to eat when I drink!'

James turned away in disgust. 'Arrgh!'

The men were about to refill their glasses when they heard the sound of boots crushing splinters behind them. Lonesome Hart looked up at the mirror behind the bottles. Even though it was cracked and stained with a lifetime of smoke tar on its surface he could make out the two men. One of them he recognized as Rawhide Jones.

'We got company, boys!' Hart announced as he took two large swallows from his potent drink before placing the glass back down. 'And I think one of them is the *hombre* we've been looking for!'

McHale was first to turn. 'Rawhide!' he gasped.

The rest of the men also turned. All

except Hart. He remained staring at the image in the distorting mirror of the man he had vowed to bury.

'You looking for me, boys?' Jones asked as he stood shoulder to shoulder with the sturdy lawman. 'Now why would ya be looking for me? I thought that even you boys would have more brains than to come after old Rawhide!'

'Weren't our idea, Rawhide! Diamond Jim sent us!' Kyle James announced fearfully.

'All of you to get one man?' Marshal Parker queried. 'I figure old Diamond Jim must not reckon any of ya chances alone, boys!'

Montana still had beer suds on his top lip. 'Who are you, old man?'

'I'm the marshal of these parts, sonny!' Parker retorted gruffly. 'It's my job to catch little children like you and take them back to the schoolmarm!'

Angrily, Montana placed his beer glass down. Again the smile had evaporated from his youthful features. He started to remove his gloves as his eyes burned across the dimly lit bar towards the sturdy figure of Parker.

'I don't cotton to fat old men with lip!' Montana snarled. 'I kinda like to shut big mouths for good!'

'I'm gonna have to tan ya hide, son!' Parker smiled. He held his Winchester across his middle and took a step forward. 'Teach ya a little respect for us old'uns!'

Rawhide Jones moved away from the marshal. His hands were hovering above the grips of his matched Colts. His eyes darted from one man to the next. Only Hart remained with his back facing him and Parker.

'Why don't ya turn around, Lonesome?'

Hart took another swallow of his hard liquor, then rested the glass down once more. He kept watching the blurred images of the two men.

'How come you got a lawman with ya, Rawhide?' Hart asked. 'You scared or something?'

'He's my deputy, boy!' Parker told him.

'Deputy!' Hart repeated the word under his breath.

James looked to Swift who looked at McHale and Montana. 'I ain't going up against the law!' James said fearfully. 'I'm not swinging on no rope even for Diamond Jim!'

'Stay where ya are!' Hart ordered.

Fear was a mighty big thing for men of James's kind. It could be the match to a fuse which could get him slapping leather to kill someone he thought was about to end his life. It could also make him walk when he knew that the odds were against his ever winning. He had walked away from many fights over the years and this was the same. He was scared. Scared of Hart but more scared of Jones and the grim-faced marshal. He knew that only a maniac drew down on the law.

He cleared his throat. 'I'm sorry, Lonesome! I'm walking out of here and heading back to Laredo!'

Hart shouted. 'Ya better not!'

James swallowed hard but kept

walking. 'If ya kill me I figure Rawhide and the marshal will have to kill you for cold-blooded murder!'

Kyle James walked between the lawmen and out into the dark street. Without a second's hesitation he pulled his reins free from the hitching rail, mounted the lathered up horse and spurred. The sound of the hoofs filled the saloon.

'Snivelling yella belly!' Hart's shoulders rose. He was angry but knew the words of the weakest member of their group were right.

Rawhide eyed the remaining men. 'Kyle said he was headed back to Laredo, boys!'

McHale nodded at Jones, the man he had known for several years. 'I reckon that's what he said OK!'

'But he headed south!' Jones smiled. 'I figure he's gonna keep riding until he's deep in the heart of Mexico! Safer than going and telling Diamond Jim about this!'

McHale raised his busy eyebrows.

'Maybe he's more scared of facing Diamond Jim than he was of arguing with Lonesome!'

'He's smart as far as I can see!' Parker drawled. 'He must have reckoned on dying here as being a real bad move! You boys got as much savvy?'

'I'm not gonna go up against the law!' Swift muttered to McHale. 'Rawhide's the law now and that's a pretty hard hand to beat! Yep! Rawhide got a full house OK!'

'Another yella belly!' Hart's head turned. His eyes glared at the smaller man and then he spat at him. Spittle hung on the face of Eli Swift. 'I thought you boys were gunfighters! I must have gotten that wrong! I've bin riding with a bunch of women!'

Swift raised a hand and wiped the spittle from his face. He lowered his head and started to follow the steps James had taken a mere few moments earlier.

'Ya coming with me, Frank?' Swift asked.

McHale looked into Rawhide's eyes and then at the marshal and his cocked Winchester. Neither man looked as though he was about to lose this fight. Then he glanced at Montana.

'C'mon, Montana! This ain't a fight we can win! Even if we did we'd be wanted and hunted like vermin! C'mon!'

At last Hart turned. His narrowed eyes watched as Swift reached his horse, then turned to look at the last two men at the crude bar beside him.

'Go on, Montana! Run away with the cowards! Show that marshal that ya are a little schoolboy like he said ya were! Go on! Run! I'll outdraw the pair of them on my own and get all the money on Rawhide's head for myself! I'll be rich! You'll be just another runt looking for an old tit to suck on!'

McHale poured himself a whiskey, downed it and rubbed his shirtsleeve across his mouth. He gave the youngest of the gunmen a look and began to walk to where he could see the mounted Swift waiting.

'Ya an old woman!' Hart called out at the oldest of the gunmen. 'Go buy yaself some wool and start knitting, Frank!'

'Better than being a dead man!' McHale said.

Parker stood firm. He heard McHale mount and spur his horse with Swift. The sound of their horses filled the street and the saloon room.

'And then there was two!' the marshal said.

Rawhide inhaled deeply. He knew that although there were only two men facing them now, one was fast and the other was reputed to be as fast or even faster than he was. Both were capable of winning this duel.

'You ought to ride, Montana!' Jones suggested. 'I don't wanna kill you! You least of all! Go on and follow the boys!'

Montana's eyes darted between Jones and the figure of Hart beside him. He did not know what to do. Then his youth and inexperience became only too apparent. The loyalty he felt for the other gunmen was one thing but the mocking words of Parker still burned in his craw. He moved closer to Hart and accepted a glass of whiskey. He tossed the strong liquor into his mouth and swallowed. His teeth gritted.

'I'm gonna stick with you, Lonesome!' Montana said. 'I fancy killing me a fat old man!'

'Good!' Hart smiled. 'I always knew that you were the only real man amongst the whole bunch!'

Montana smiled again. It was the smile of a boy who thought that because he could kill like a man he was a man.

'Lawmen or no lawmen, I'll match ya shot for shot!'

Hart patted the youngster's shoulder. 'I'm proud of ya, Montana! Only a man can stand firm like you are doing with me!'

Jones was uneasy.

'Ya making a big mistake, Montana!'

'And so are you, Rawhide!' Montana smiled.

'The difference is that I know it!' Jones said.

'Don't be feared of Rawhide's words, Montana!' Hart told the youngster. 'That's all they are! Words!'

An unholy rumble seemed to sweep over Santa Maria as black clouds crashed into one another. The storm had arrived far sooner than any of them had expected. It sounded as though a hundred ghosts were fighting for supremacy in the turbulent heavens above them.

Then the whole town shook. A massive explosion above them rocked the very ground they stood upon. Rain like a bursting dam suddenly poured straight down. Every drop bounced ten feet high off the sun-hardened sand. A blinding flash of light illuminated the entire street.

Satan had decided the fight should start.

The four men inside the saloon obeyed.

144

18

The two lawmen were taken by surprise.. Neither Rawhide Jones nor Ethan Parker had ever seen such speed as Hart's hands snapped both his Colts from their holsters and started firing. Red-hot shafts of lead cut across the saloon. The two lanterns propped on the bar counter were first to taste the deadly accuracy of bullets which came from Lonesome Hart's guns.

The room was immediately plunged into darkness. Its only illumination was from the storm that was raging out in the street. As soon as the ferocity of the storm had shaken the adobe walls of the saloon and distracted both Parker and Jones, Lonesome Hart had realized that it was his best opportunity to act. Perhaps it was his only chance to get the better of the men with stars pinned to their shirts.

He had drawn with a speed that even Jones would have been proud of.

After killing the feeble light and without a thought for the young man who stood beside him, the tall murderous gunfighter had holstered one of his guns, grabbed Montana around the neck and dragged the stunned youngster in front of his chest.

Montana had become his human shield and would not be released until he had served his purpose. Montana would soak up the bullets aimed at Hart himself from his adversaries' weaponry.

With the gun in his free hand Hart blasted at the pair of lawmen who, he knew, were somewhere close. Montana struggled but could do nothing as the far stronger Hart squeezed the life from the young gunman in his grip.

Hart's grip was so strong that he felt and heard the neck of the young gunfighter snap like a dried twig. The tall man dropped his gun hand and flipped the planks off the barrels. He moved steadily backward as bullets continued to plunge into Montana's lifeless torso.

The storm continued to rage over Santa Maria but its rage was nothing compared to that which had enshrouded the saloon.

With the lightning forking down all around the small town and rain battering everything beneath the vicious storm clouds the two remaining gun-fighters' horses tugged and fought to be released from the hitching rails which held them in check.

Jones had thrown himself to the floor when Hart had started firing his guns. Feverishly he had fanned the hammer of one of his Colts, unaware that the bullets intended for Hart were actually finding Montana instead.

At the same moment that Jones had landed on the floor of the pitch-black room, Parker had dropped on to one knee and started firing his Winchester to where he had last seen Hart standing.

The sound of bottles shattering filled their ears.

The brief flashes of light as gun hammers struck bullet casings, sending their lethal lead spewing from smoking barrels, were not enough for any of them to see their targets. Acrid smoke from guns and rifle only hindered the narrowed eyes of the three men as they vainly tried to see.

Knowing that Hart's bullets were getting too close, Rawhide Jones scrambled to the cover of an upturned table and shook his spent shells from his gun as he kept firing his other weapon.

'You dead yet, Rawhide?' Hart screamed over the noise of the storm and the bullets which kept homing in on him. Every bullet that hit the dead youngster propped up before him punched the gunfighter further backwards.

Jones did not reply with words. He let his Colt do his talking as he kept moving from one side to the other. The red-hot tapers were still cutting across the room at him and the kneeling marshal.

With a bravery seldom seen anywhere Parker ignored the red fireflies of lead as they passed all around him. He just cranked and fired his rifle into the darkest parts of the saloon.

'Ya not even getting close, boys!' Hart called out.

'I must have hit one of them!' the confused marshal exclaimed. 'I ain't that bad a shot!'

'You ain't, Ethan!' Jones placed one gun at his knees and pulled bullets from his belt. He reloaded one pistol, holstered it and then repeated the action with the other. 'Lonesome's up to something!'

Suddenly there was a lull. Hart had stopped shooting.

Parker crawled quickly across the stale sawdust to his deputy and cranked the mechanism of his rifle again. Somehow their eyes had adjusted to the darkness.

'You hit, boy?'

'Not yet!'

'Why do ya figure they've quit shooting?'

Jones moved his head closer to the gruff voice. 'I don't think that Montana's fired one shot, Marshal!'

Parker licked his dry lips. 'Ya don't? How come?'

'I think that ornery bastard Hart is using the kid to hide behind!' Jones replied. 'I'm sure I seen him grab Montana a split second after he shot the lanterns out!'

'That could be why I ain't dropped him!' Parker said. 'I'm sure my bullets have bin on target! If'n ya right that explains why he's still standing!'

The room remained silent.

What neither lawman knew was that Hart had dragged Montana's bullet-riddled corpse to the furthest corner of the saloon and swapped his empty gun for the one in Montana's holster. He had noticed a door in the shadows as soon as he and the other men had first entered the saloon. Where it led he did not know, but it gave him an escape route should he require it. Hart laboured with the dead weight of the limp body in his arms and moved to the door. He tried its handle. It was locked.

'Did ya hear that?' Jones asked the marshal quietly.

'Yep!' The marshal answered, 'Spurs being dragged across the floor and a door handle being turned! Damn it, Rawhide! Ya right! That stinking bastard must have used the young'un to soak up our lead! He's still hiding behind him!'

Both men knew that they had to attempt to end this now. It was kill or be killed.

Jones held a gun in each hand. His thumbs cocked both their hammers back until they fully locked. He took a deep breath.

'You ready to open up with everything we got left, Ethan?'

'Ya damn right, boy!' Parker answered.

'On the count of three we rise and start shooting!' Jones suggested.

'Between us we can spray bullets across the entire back wall! One of us ought to get lucky!'

Parker held his rifle firmly. 'Count!'

Jones counted. 'One, two, three!'

Both men stood. Both men started to fire. Bullets were returned. Suddenly they both heard a hollow cry come from behind them. Even the deafening thunderclaps and gunplay could not disguise the sound of someone being hit.

Instinctively Parker knew who had made such a pitiful noise as Hart's lead cut into him. The marshal swung around. He was just in time to see one of his beloved sons buckle and drop in the doorway.

'Walking Lion!'

Then, as he started to run to his son, another of Hart's bullets found his broad back. He was knocked off his feet by the sheer impact. Parker hit the ground face first. He skidded and crashed into the body. Rain cascaded down over them both but only Ethan

Parker seemed to be still moving.

'Marshal?' Jones called back as he stared in disbelief at the two crumpled figures. Then a shot came close. Too close. It tore through his shirt and he buckled as he felt a rib shatter. He managed to return fire. Both his Colts spat their venom back at Hart.

A scream came from the shadows.

This time Jones knew he had found his elusive target.

Lonesome Hart kicked the back door down with a single strike of one of his boots. Light from the flashing sky illuminated his figure as he fled out into the storm.

Jones blasted his weapons again and went to follow. A pain like none he had ever experienced before ripped through him like a branding-iron.

He staggered and dropped down in the middle of the saloon floor. He glanced at the rear door and the lashing rain before he turned to look at the saloon porch. He somehow managed to holster one of his guns, then crawled back to where the two men were lying in the pouring rain.

Rawhide Jones had seen both men fall. He paused, touched his side and felt the sharp bone that protruded from his flesh. Blood covered his fingertips.

'What happened, Rawhide?' Painted Tail shouted down at the kneeling man as he reached the saloon porch and saw the sickening spectacle. 'What happened to my father and brother?'

Blood was everywhere. Even the rain could not wash it away as fast as it flowed from the three men on the ground.

Rawhide Jones looked up at the bedraggled Painted Tail and saw the pain etched into his handsome features.

'We got ourselves shot, son!'

'Who did this?'

'His name's Lonesome Hart!' Jones muttered.

Painted Tail dropped down into the blood and started to examine both the marshal and Walking Lion. Steam rose from both the unmoving bodies. Jones crawled closer and then realized the youth was crying.

'I think that they are dead, Rawhide!'

With the torrential rain filling his eyes Jones ignored his own agony. He sighed, reached out and tried to find signs of life on the pair of fallen men. His search was in vain. All his hands could locate was death.

He looked at Painted Tail. 'I reckon ya might be right!'

19

The floor of the doctor's office was wet with a mixture of rainwater and blood. Rawhide Jones stared in disbelief at the two bodies stretched out in the doctor's office. He had seen a lot of death in his life but it had not prepared him for this. This was the result of pure evil. Father and son had been slain by one of Brady's deadliest recruits. It sickened him. The young Walking Lion could have not been more than twenty and yet one bullet had ended his brief existence. Marshal Ethan Parker had been a sturdy man who seemed the sort who would never fall foul of anyone's bullet and yet he too lay completely motionless. The stars on their shirts glinted in the lamplight.

Painted Tail had not spoken a word since he and Jones had carried the two bodies through the driving rain to the doctor's home on the edge of town. Now he stood staring down at what was left of his father and brother.

He was like a statue. Unblinking yet noble and unable to accept his loss.

'Who done this terrible thing?' Doc Harper asked as he dried his hands on a towel and moved slowly back across the wet boards to the bodies and two silent men.

'A man named Lonesome Hart, Doc!' Jones replied. 'Reckoned to be a gunfighter but as far as I'm concerned he's just a low-down back-shooter!'

'Why? This is the handiwork of an outlaw, not a gunslinger!' said Harper sorrowfully. 'No one shoots lawmen like this unless they got themselves a reason!'

Jones glanced at the medical man. 'I'm starting to wonder about that myself, Doc! Maybe Lonesome is an outlaw!'

Harper put his fingers to his lips and then looked Jones straight in the eyes.

'What ya say his name is?'

'They call him Lonesome Hart, Doc!' Jones answered. 'Why do ya want to know?'

Harper's eyes tightened around its wrinkles. 'Was he ever in Santa Maria before? Like maybe a month or so back?'

Jones nodded. 'Yep! I heard him tell Brady about being down here around then! What ya getting at?'

'Is he tall? I mean even taller than you?'

Again Jones nodded. 'Yep!'

Harper snapped his fingers. 'That's it! He must be the varmint who back-shot our sheriff!'

Rawhide Jones exhaled heavily. 'The filthy bastard! Diamond Jim must have known that Hart was a killer when he hired him! I figure he needed a back-shooter to execute all the shady deals he's bin coming up with of late!'

'He work for Diamond Jim Brady?' Painted Tail growled in a hushed tone. 'Bad like outlaw! Painted Tail track and kill Lonesone Hart! Kill him the

Cheyenne way! Slow! Very slow!'

Jones swallowed hard. He walked the few steps to the youngster with the long, raven-black hair and placed a hand upon his shoulder.

'Easy, son! We'll both bring Hart to justice!'

Painted Tail looked into the eyes of the man who still wore the deputy star his father had given him.

'No take easy, Rawhide! No let bad men live for this! Hart and Brady die the Cheyenne way!'

Jones nodded. 'Your father said we could go into Laredo and arrest anyone as long as we wear these stars!'

'Yes, Rawhide! We can arrest or we can kill! Painted Tail choose to kill!'

Jones wanted to argue but he felt exactly the same. He knew that they had the law on their side. They could go back to Laredo and kill Lonesome Hart and the man he worked for without anyone raising a finger to stop them. Hart had killed two lawmen and wounded another. Brady had sent him here and that made him eligible for the noose as well.

That was enough.

Jones was about to speak when he felt a pain in his side. He looked down and saw the doctor's fingers touching the strapping he had applied only a few minutes earlier.

'That still hurts, huh?' Harper asked.

'Yep!' Jones sighed. 'It still hurts a lot! Especially when someone pokes at it, Doc!'

'I'll strap ya up a tad tighter, boy!' Harper went to his bag and pulled out a roll of bandages. 'I figure you and ya young pal are intending going riding!'

Jones nodded. 'Yeah! Me and Painted Tail got business in Laredo!'

'I'll strap ya real tight!' The doctor sighed. 'We don't want that rib to bust out again, do we?'

Rawhide Jones looked at the young man and then back at Harper.

'Ya right, Doc! Strap it up real tight! Me and my fellow deputy got us a whole lotta riding to do before this is over!'

20

The rider had left the storm far behind him. Yet he continued to whip the shoulders of the mount he had stolen back at Santa Maria as he drove across the sand towards the outskirts of Laredo. He was like a man waiting for death to strike out at him at any moment. Hours earlier, before dawn, he had somehow managed to navigate a safe route through the canyon without arousing the wrath of the Apaches. But it was not the thought of the Apaches that kept Lonesome Hart whipping his horse. It was the man named Rawhide Jones he feared.

Few men had ever had the courage to stand his ground and match bullet for bullet with Hart. Jones had done just that and it haunted him.

Blood covered the shoulders of the flagging horse as it vainly tried to outrun the long leather reins as they continued to punish it.

The sun was high and its merciless rays blazed down on the arid land and the horseman who drove the mount on and on ferociously beneath him.

Hart kept forcing the animal to find a pace which would eventually kill it. He was in a rush to escape the demons he had unleashed from Pandora's box back at Santa Maria. Men like Jones did not start fights but Hart knew that they often finished them.

A cloud of dust swirled from the hoofs of the horse as it finally reached the end of its strength. Laredo was busy as the horseman rode into its southern-most streets astride the staggering animal.

Hart spurred hard but the horse was spent. It had nothing left after running throughout the long night and half a day's span.

There was no sight worse than a valiant horse dying. It fell heavily just as it reached Krell's livery stable and its

162

large corral. Lonesome Hart was thrown over the head and neck of the pitiful creature. He rolled several times before being stopped by a large water barrel outside the livery building.

He sat up and stared at the bullet hole in his right leg as it pumped blood through his torn pants' leg. He tried to tighten the bandanna he had tied around his lean thigh but it was wet with gore.

Harvey Krell walked out into the sunlight and stared at the gunfighter and the animal he had destroyed. He said nothing as Hart scrambled to his feet and pulled one of his guns from its holster. Then Hart aimed and fired at the head of the shaking horse.

The horse's skull shattered.

'What ya looking at, Krell?' Hart spat.

'Nothing, Mr Hart!' The stableman replied. 'Never easy to put a horse out of its agony!'

'Saddle me one of ya nags and be quick about it!' Hart demanded as he slid the smoking gun back, into its leather holster. 'Send the bill to Brady! He owes me for this leg!'

'Who shot ya?'

'I ain't sure, it was kinda dark!'

'Weren't Rawhide Jones, was it?'

Hart glared at the old-timer who still had more muscles than most men half his age. He spat again. A lump of brown goo landed at Krell's feet.

'Do what ya told, Krell!'

Krell nodded and opened the gate of the corral. Half a dozen animals roamed around inside the fenced-off area. He walked into it, grabbed the bridle of the slowest of his stock and led it out into the wide street.

'I ain't got me a spare saddle, Mr Hart!'

'Use the one on that lump of glue!' Hart pointed at the dead horse between them.

Krell nodded again. He laboured at pulling the saddle from the dead animal. His well-toned muscles soon achieved their mission, though. He threw the saddle and blanket over the back of the horse and bent down to take hold of the cinch straps. Krell lifted the blood-covered fender and hooked its stirrup over the blood-splattered saddle horn.

'You seen any signs of McHale or Swift?' Hart asked as he stared down the long main street to Brady's distant house.

'Nope!' Krell replied as he secured the cinch. 'Ain't seen any of Diamond Jim's boys until you showed up!'

Hart walked to the older man and took the reins of the fresh mount. He stepped in the stirrup and hoisted his aching bones up into the saddle. His wounded leg seemed stiff to the old stableman.

'You're shot, Mr Hart!'

'I already figured that, Krell!' Hart spat. 'Maybe it was the bullet hole in my leg that gave it away!'

'Ya ought to find a doctor to sew ya up!' Krell advised. 'I seen men lose legs with the gangrene!'

'I got me more important business to sort out first!'

Harvey Krell watched as the gunfighter spurred and rode off towards his paymaster's home.

This time it was Krell's time to spit. 'I sure hope ya die slow, Mr Hart! Running a horse to death like ya done here oughta be a hanging offence!'

Hart knew that there was still a slim chance of collecting on the reward Diamond Jim had placed upon the head of Rawhide Jones. All he had to do was wait for him to show up in Laredo and finish the job he had started the previous night.

He knew that Jones would follow. For men like Jones wanted justice above all else. Hart had killed two of the men who stood with Rawhide Jones and he was certain the man would follow to seek vengeance.

Even Rawhide Jones could not turn his back on revenge. His sort were spurred on by an unwriiten code. Jones would have to try and avenge the death of the men Hart had dispatched back at Santa Maria.

Hart rode hard along the main street. His eyes were screwed up until they were just a pair of slits carved into his face. He saw only the large house where he knew Brady would be waiting for him. People had to run out of the way as the wide-eyed horse thundered along the busy thoroughfare, trying to escape the rider's spurs.

As the horseman neared the grandiose building he began to try and think of an excuse for why he did not have the body of Rawhide Jones in tow.

He had to lie and lie big.

When you did business with folks like Brady you had to put on an act so they did not turn upon you. Hart knew that if Rawhide Jones had been capable of lying as well as he could, Diamond Jim would have forgiven him anything.

But men like Rawhide Jones were just too honest.

Hart hauled back on his reins and stopped the horse at the gates of the mansion built by a man who had managed to trick his way to unimaginable wealth.

He carefully dropped down to the sand and felt his leg squirt even more of his blood away in the process. He gritted his teeth and marched without limping towards the hand-carved door.

At least he could prove he had been in a gun battle, he thought. The bullet and the blood-soaked pants' leg were proof of that.

Lonesome Hart pulled one of his guns from its holster and started to pound upon the door. He could hear the echo coming from inside the vast interior.

Then he saw something to his left.

Something which surprised and angered him.

Two familiar horses, belonging to Frank McHale and Eli Swift, were tied up in the courtyard in the shade of a withered tree.

They had arrived here before him, Hart told himself. What lies had they already poured into Diamond Jim Brady's ears? The question burned even more ferociously than the hole in his right thigh.

Again he pounded the gun against the door. Splinters fell from its hand-carved façade.

'Open up!' Hart yelled out.

He dropped the gun back into its resting-place on his hip. He had never imagined that they would return here after running away from the fight with Jones.

'Open this damn door!'

Then Hart heard the sound of the massive bolts barring the solid wooden door being released. He then watched as the door began to be opened by one of Brady's many servants.

'Get out of my way!' Hart spat. He pushed the small man aside and screamed. 'Diamond Jim! Ya got them stinking cowards in here with ya?'

The servant watched as the raging Lonesome Hart limped into the house. The small man followed fearfully as the wounded gunfighter searched for the men he knew were somewhere within the great mansion.

A trail of blood gleamed on the marble flooring with every step Hart took.

'Where are ya?'

Then to one side he saw movement out of the corner of his eye. Hart turned and stared. Brady walked with a cup in his left hand as his right remained a few inches from his gun grip.

'What are you saying, Lonesome?' Brady asked.

'I got me a score to settle with them bastards, Diamond Jim!' Lonesome Hart screamed out. The threats echoed all around the many rooms of the house. 'They left me and Montana to be cut down by a bunch of lawmen!'

Brady blew into the cup. Steam rose and filled the hall with the aroma of coffee.

'You thirsty?'

'Yep!' Hart snarled. 'Thirsty for their blood!'

21

'Them's mighty big words for a man bleeding like a stuck pig, Lonesome!' Frank McHale's voice boomed out from above Hart and the silent Brady.

'Ya want our blood?' Eli Swift asked. 'Then ya gotta fight to get it!'

McHale and Swift suddenly appeared at the top of the grand staircase beyond the two men. They started to walk down towards the marble-floored hall. Both men, had their coats pushed back over their holstered gun grips.

'So there ya are!' Hart said loudly.

Neither gunman spoke until they both reached the foot of the staircase. They just kept their eyes fixed on the wounded Hart as their hands twitched above the grips of their weapons.

'So Montana's dead, huh?' Swift asked.

'Ya should have left the boy to ride

with us, Lonesome!' McHale growled. 'He was too green to face Rawhide!'

'He might have bin green but he was more of a man than either of you two!' Hart raged. 'He didn't run away when he saw the stars pinned on them varmints! You just wet ya pants and ran away!'

McHale stood firm a few feet away from Swift. Both men had their hands poised above their guns. Both men knew what it meant to risk everything on the speed of their hands and accuracy of their aim.

'Ya never gonna outdraw me!' Hart warned.

'Maybe!' McHale said.

Brady continued to sip at his steaming beverage. 'If any of you start shooting in here I'll be damn angry!' he muttered.

'But they run out on me and Montana, Mr Brady!' Hart said through gritted teeth.

'And they're in one piece and you got a hole in ya!' Brady observed loudly. 'I want you all to relax and lower them gun hands! Now!'

Slowly the three men obeyed.

McHale and Swift touched the brims of their hats and moved off into another part of the vast house. Hart eased his tall frame around until he was square on to his boss. He was about to speak when his and Brady's attention was diverted.

There was panic in the voice of the small servant as he raced through the hall towards his master and the gunfighter who stood in a pool of his own blood. Diamond Jim Brady glanced up from the cup at his lips to look at the panting man.

'Señor Jim! Señor Jim!' The frightened man kept repeating as he reached the seemingly emotionless figure.

'What, Luis?' Brady asked calmly.

The servant was shaking and pointing back at the open door forty feet behind him.

'Two men come into town! I see them as I was going to close the door!'

173

'So?' Brady finished his coffee and placed the cup down on a side table.

'One is Señor Rawhide and the other is an Indian!' Luis Garcia gasped.

Brady's face seemed to drain of all its colour. His mind raced as he swallowed hard and patted the servant on his thin shoulder.

'Thank you, Luis!'

'Rawhide and a stinking Injun?' Hart limped to the gambler and rubbed the trail dust from his whiskered features. 'What in tarnation is that old man doing with an Injun?'

'So Frank and Eli were right! They figured you wouldn't be able to finish Rawhide off!' Brady began to walk along the corridor towards the sunlight which flowed in unchecked through the open doorway.

'Rawhide weren't alone!' Hart snapped as he limped behind Brady. 'Them boys back there high-tailed it and left me and little Montana to take them on alone! I got two of the bastards but was plugged and had to get out of there!'

'And Montana?'

'Rawhide killed him in cold blood!'

'I got a few problems with your story, Lonesome!'

'Them cowards have poisoned ya mind against me, Mr Brady!' Hart said. 'I stood up and tried to follow ya orders but they chickened out! That's the truth!'

'The thing is I've known Rawhide for about five years and he ain't never killed anyone in cold blood!' Brady said bluntly. 'I wish he had but it just ain't in his nature!'

'He killed Montana!' Hart repeated.

Brady paused, rested a hand against the white-washed wall and stared out across Laredo like a monarch surveying all he possessed. He could see the pair of horse-men outside the distant livery stable. He recognized the tall black stallion before his eyes made out the animal's master.

'That's Rawhide!' Brady sighed. 'Who do you figure that Indian is?'

'There was another Injun with Rawhide and the marshal!' Hart spat out into the courtyard. 'I killed him! Maybe there was two of the critters working for that marshal!'

Brady glanced briefly at Hart. 'You sure do like killing folks with stars on their chests, don't you?'

'I told ya that myself, Diamond Jim!' Hart snorted angrily.

Brady stared at the man who was still bleeding. Only a month earlier he had thought that he had hired the perfect replacement for Rawhide Jones but now he doubted his own judgement.

'I'll get someone to run for the doctor and fix that leg of yours up, Lonesome!' Brady turned and signalled to the little servant who was still hovering in the large hallway. 'Go get the Doc, Luis! Tell him we got us a wounded man here!'

The servant ran between the two men standing in the frame of the door and down into the dusty streets.

'I ain't got time to be sewn up, Mr Brady! I got me some more killing to do!'

Diamond Jim Brady sighed. 'You got the time! Rawhide don't seem to be in any hurry to ride up here, Lonesome! Maybe he's getting second thoughts of facing you again!'

Hart pulled out his tobacco and bit off a chunk. He started to chew as his eyes remained glued to the distant horsemen.

★ ★ ★

More than two hours had passed by since the two horsemen had arrived in Laredo and stopped their mounts outside the livery stable. Rawhide Jones and Painted Tail remained in the shade of the building as Harvey Krell watered, fed and rubbed down their mounts, Neither of the deputies had taken their eyes from the house where Diamond Jim Brady held court like a king from some ancient land. They had seen the doctor go there and return to his office as they ate their jerky and hard tack before washing it down with some of

Krell's infamous coffee. Nothing escaped their trained eyes as they rested.

Eventually Krell walked out into the fresh air and breathed deeply to get the smell of horses out of his flared nostrils. He glanced at the two men who were sitting on the hard ground with their backs against the front wall of his livery. The only thing they seemed to have in common was the tin stars they both wore proudly upon their shirts.

'Good coffee, Harvey!' Jones said.

'It's all in the grounds, boy!'

Jones nodded. 'Maybe!'

Krell walked and then stopped to look down at the only man in Laredo whom he actually trusted. He leaned down and squinted.

'You wounded, Rawhide?' Krell asked as he accepted a cigar from Jones.

Jones looked up at the liveryman's wrinkled face as he sucked on the fresh cigar in his mouth. For a moment he thought that Krell must have developed the power of mind-reading, then he realized his shirt still bore the evidence of the broken rib, shattered when one of Hart's bullets had skidded off his side. A tear and dried blood covered more than a quarter of the once new shirt.

'I'm OK!' Jones said, lighting his cigar. 'Got me a rib shot up. That's all!'

'Ya sure are in better shape than Lonesome, Rawhide!' Krell leaned over and accepted the flame to the tip of his cigar. He puffed and winked. 'That boy was pumping blood all over the place! Fell off his horse and then shot the dumb critter!'

The two deputies both looked at the dead horse a few yards from where they were seated. It was now drawing flies.

'Lonesome sure has had himself some real bad luck lately, Harvey!' Jones said through a cloud of smoke.

'I sure hope that you boys can add to that tally!' Krell chuckled. 'I hopes ya kill him!'

Jones inhaled smoke. 'So do I!'

'I kill Lonesome Hart, old man!'

Painted Tail said. 'I kill him Cheyenne way!'

'Somebody oughta!' Krell nodded.

Rawhide eased himself back to his full height and brushed the dust from his pants with gloved hands. The youngster jumped up intending to go into the livery where their mounts were. Jones placed a hand across the chest of Painted Tail and shook his head.

'Wait, my friend!' Jones said in a low soft tone.

Painted Tail stopped. 'I wait!'

Krell raised a hand and shielded his eyes from the bright sun. He kept looking at something halfway down the long main street.

'Well I'll be!'

'What ya seen, Harvey?' Jones asked.

'A mighty fancy buggy,' Krell answered. 'That belongs to the new mayor of this fine city, boy.'

'Proctor?'

'Yep!'

Jones narrowed his own eyes. 'What's he doing riding around at this hour? He don't usually rise before dark, as I recall!'

Krell laughed. 'Yep! He's a real politician and no mistake!'

'When we go to kill bad men, Rawhide?' Painted Tail asked anxiously.

Both men looked at the handsome youngster who continued to stare with unblinking eyes at the house where they all knew Hart and Brady were.

Jones tapped Krell on the arm. 'Go get our horses, Harvey!'

Krell nodded.

'We go now?' Painted Tail asked Jones.

'Yep!' Rawhide Jones confirmed.

Finale

Along with a thousand others, Krell watched the two riders as they rode down the long main street towards the place where they intended to administer their own individual brands of justice. Rawhide Jones knew that grief could sway even the most level-headed of men and he worried about the young rider beside him. Would Painted Tail Parker be able to control the rage which was brewing within his whole being? It was a question that Jones knew he was unable to answer.

Both horsemen could see the activity up at the big house as they drew closer and closer to their goal. Then everything outside the house went quiet. It was obvious that Brady wanted to confine the actions of his men to its interior, away from prying eyes.

Regardless of what lay in the near

future the horsemen kept riding and praying to their individual gods for guidance.

Jones leaned on his saddle horn. He could see the buggy that he knew belonged to the mayor standing just outside the gates of Brady's impressive home. But he had no time to wonder why Proctor was there. All he could think of was Brady and Hart.

As the riders reached the high walls that surrounded the house and its large courtyard, Painted Tail suddenly got up on to the back of his pony and stood, just in time to grab at an overhanging branch of a tall tree which had its roots firmly embedded inside the boundaries of the property.

With the agility of a mountain lion the youngster lifted himself up and disappeared into the leafy canopy.

Jones gasped and was about to speak. He remained silent when he saw what Painted Tail was doing. He watched in stunned awe as his fellow deputy dropped down on to the top of the high wall and ran along it towards the rear of the building.

He eased back on his reins and stroked the neck of the black stallion. He was now only ten feet from the wide gateway. Again he glanced at the buggy, now with its back to him.

It was impossible to determine whether Mayor Proctor was in the vehicle from the place where his mount stood. Again he raised his eyes to the high wall and he wondered where his companion had gone. He had hoped the youth would stand beside him when the shooting started but now he knew he had to face Brady and what remained of his henchmen alone.

He inhaled deeply and tapped his spurs.

'C'mon, Jet!'

The stallion walked around the corner of the high wall and moved closer to the mansion's showy facade. Jones's eyes flashed from window to window. Corner to corner. He could not see anyone.

The horseman stopped his stallion. He dismounted, then adjusted his gunbelt and flicked the small safety loops off the two gun hammers.

Although the house appeared quiet Jones knew that, like everything else Diamond Jim Brady had ever had anything to do with, that was an illusion.

The seasoned Rawhide Jones had to ensure it would not prove to be a deadly one.

He walked slowly away from his horse towards the front door. His hands hovered above the grips of his holstered Colts. Then, as he was a mere two steps from the door, he heard its bolts being released.

Jones stopped.

The door was pulled open to reveal the small servant he had known for half a decade. The man was shaking with fear, unable to conceal his terror.

'Señor Rawhide!'

'Luis!' Jones replied.

The small man gestured toward the

depths of the cavernous interior of the building. 'Señor Jim wait for you!'

Jones stepped closer and leaned down. 'He alone?'

Although Luis Garcia did not answer with words, his head gave the slightest of shakes. He was trying to warn the man with the deputy marshal's star that death awaited somewhere within the buildings many rooms.

Sweat was pouring down the servant's face as he vainly tried to hold on to the door with hands that refused to stop trembling.

'Run, Luis!' Jones whispered. 'Run for your life!'

The servant did not need to be told twice. He fled like a man who knew what was about to happen.

Rawhide Jones licked his dry lips and began to walk deeper into the cool house. His spurs signalled his every stride upon the marble flooring, upon which he could see the dried droplets of blood, which were everywhere.

When he had walked about thirty feet

into the hall a voice called out from one of the many rooms. It was Brady's voice.

'C'mon in, Rawhide!' it invited. 'You ain't got nothing to be afraid of! I'm alone!'

Jones crouched down and carefully removed each of his spurs as quietly as he could. He then rose up to his full height with them in his hands.

'Don't tell me that my top gunfighter's scared?' Brady laughed out loud.

'I've come to arrest you and Lonesome, Diamond Jim!' Jones called back. 'There's a couple of ropes waiting for you both back in Santa Maria!'

'I don't think I'll oblige you, Rawhide!' Brady's voice had changed. It no longer had any humour in it. 'I'm not going any place!'

Jones started to walk again. This time his spurs did not betray him. Then, when he was a mere six feet from the open doorway he tossed the spurs at its frame.

A volley of bullets came from the

room and hit both the spurs before they had reached the floor. The deafening sound of gunfire filled the house.

With both guns drawn Rawhide Jones threw himself on to the marble floor and slid across it. When he reached the open doorway he saw the four men. They all had smoking guns in their hands.

McHale and Swift were standing before Brady whilst Hart was seated in a corner. Brady was close to an open window about thirty feet away.

The gunmen started to fire their guns again. Frank McHale fanned his gun hammer furiously whilst Eli Swift seemed to be rationing his bullets. Chippings of marble were torn from the surface of the floor.

Jones squeezed the triggers of both his Colts.

McHale was hit dead centre. Lifted off his feet, he crashed down on the large oak desk. Swift was caught low and buckled, as he felt the lead drive into him. He landed on his knees and stared with disbelieving eyes at his own reflection in the marble.

Before Jones could scramble to his feet he saw Diamond Jim Brady leap out of the open window. The deputy fired but his bullet only shattered one of the window's many panes.

Lonesome Hart stood with his guns levelled at Jones.

'Better stop that gunplay, Rawhide!' Hart warned. 'Or I'll kill ya right now!'

Jones lowered his hands. The smoke drifted up from their barrels as he got back on his feet.

'Why don't ya just shoot, Lonesome?'

Hart smirked and spat a lump of brown spittle at the floor between them. He then limped closer to the man he hated.

'Yeah! Maybe I oughta just shoot ya, old-timer!' he snarled.

The wounded Eli Swift was on his knees, mumbling as blood dripped from his mouth.

Hart levelled one of his guns at the gunfighter on the floor, then squeezed its trigger. The bullet took Swift's head almost clean off. What remained of the man crumpled.

'Ya must be over the hill, Rawhide!' Hart sneered. 'Leaving a man to suffer like that! I was told that when ya killed ya done it clean!'

Jones bit his lower lip. 'You could be right!'

'Holster them hoglegs and we'll see who is the fastest!' Hart steadied himself. 'That's if ya got the belly for a real showdown! Have ya?'

Jones did not reply. He silently dropped both guns into their holsters, tilted his head and just stared at the man opposite him.

'Ya ready, old man?' Hart leered and holstered his weapons. 'Ya ready to die?'

'Yep!' Jones replied drily.

Suddenly a noise from the open window drew their gaze. It was the spine-chilling call of a young man with Cheyenne blood flowing through his veins. Painted Tail unleashed his anger and with all his strength threw his knife.

The sunlight flashed across its honed blade as it carved through the air. Hart shook from the impact of the knife and then staggered backwards. The entire blade had gone into his chest right up to its hilt.

Before Lonesome Hart fell Painted Tail had leapt into the room and was upon him.

Rawhide Jones screwed up his eyes and gritted his teeth. He knew the young man would be true to his word. He would kill Hart the Cheyenne way.

Another noise came from the open window. This time it was the unmistakable sound of a horse out in the courtyard. Jones knew the sound of his prized stallion. He also knew that Diamond Jim Brady was just smart enough to know that if he were to take the black stallion there was no other horse in five counties that could catch it.

Feverishly Jones ran along the marble flooring towards the open front door.

He saw Brady clambering up into the saddle of his black stallion. A shot came from Brady's gun and hit the door a few inches to the side of Jones's head.

Burning splinters exploded from the woodwork and filled his eyes. He dropped to one knee and desperately tried to rid his eyes of the agony.

The horse was turned and Brady kicked the stallion hard. The mount began to run towards the gateway. Then, as the sight returned to one of Jones's eyes, he saw Mayor Elias Proctor lean out from the cover of his buggy with a gun in his hand.

Two shots rang out.

Diamond Jim Brady was punched off the saddle by the sheer force of the well-placed lead. He hit the ground hard and did not move again.

'Why did ya help me, Mr Mayor?' Jones asked as he walked past the body to the man seated in the buggy. 'I don't understand!'

'I didn't help you, Deputy!' Proctor

answered. 'I helped myself and the rest of Laredo!'

The smartly dressed mayor slapped his reins down on the back of his horse and steered the buggy full circle.

Rawhide Jones watched the buggy as it made its way back down the long street. He rubbed his eyes again and then saw his young companion walking out from the house with the bloody knife in his hand. Painted Tail paused, slid the knife into its leather scabbard on his belt and then nodded.

'The Cheyenne way!' he said.

Rawhide Jones nodded. 'Yep! The Cheyenne way!'

THE END

LAST MILE TO NOGALES

Ryan Bodie

Nogales was a hell town, in the heart of the desert. Its single claim to fame was its band of deadly guns-for-hire who lived there, especially Ryan Coder, whom some saw as the gun king. Yet Coder found his life on the line when he hired out to the king of Chad Valley and was pitted against Holly, the youngest and deadliest gunslinger of them all. Would Coder end up just another notch on Holly's gun?

THE DEVIL'S RIDER

Lance Howard

When vicious outlaw Jeremy Trask escapes the hangman's noose, he rides into Baton Ridge on a mission of revenge and bloodlust. It had been a year since he'd murdered manhunter Jim Darrow's brother in cold blood. Now, along with the sole survivor of the massacre, a young homeless widow named Spring Treller, Darrow vows to hunt down the outlaw — this time to finish him for good. But will he survive the deadly reception the outlaw has waiting?

SHOWDOWN AT PAINTED ROCK

Walt Masterson

When a wagon train is trapped by armed men in Painted Desert, mountain man Obadiah Peabody helps out. He believes they are all just another bunch of pilgrims aiming for California. But among the innocent travellers are the Driscoll brothers — the meanest bunch of owlhoots. Obadiah realises he's got a tiger by the tail when the brothers turn on their rescuer and kidnap his adopted granddaughter. Can Obadiah succeed against seemingly impossible odds? Can he even survive?

MISFIT LIL CLEANS UP

Chap O'Keefe

A senseless killing prevents scout and guide Jackson Farraday from investigating an odd situation in the Black Dog mining settlement. So he tricks Lilian Goodnight into spying at the High Meadows cattle ranch. Lil discovers range boss Liam O'Grady running a haywire outfit, crewed by deep-dyed misfits. She then finds she must rescue an ex-British army officer, Albert Fitzcuthbert, from renegade Indians. And Lil faces ever more problems that only her savvy, daring and guns can settle!

RANGELAND RUCKUS

Randall Sawka

Chet Mitchell's dream was to raise cattle, near the town of Tanning, in a seemingly inaccessible valley. However, landowner Dave Tanning didn't want strangers to ranch land that he felt belonged to his family. And people laughed at Chet's plan to access the valley, which was surrounded by mountains and enormous rock walls. Many had tried, and died. But when Mitchell unveiled his surprise, Dave Tanning had to face a man who knew how to use his head and his guns . . .

s . : r : r a r a e a l l h